BREAKING THE WISHBONE

Praise for *Breaking the Wishbone*

'The story is beautifully written. Its shape
and structure work perfectly, and give each character a
chance to tell it like it is for them personally. It is full of
insights into life on the street, but does
not overwhelm with horror.'

Julie Parsons, author of *Mary, Mary* and *The Courtship Gift*

'This is exactly how young people out-of-home are, how they
sound, how they react, how they cope with their situation,
living in a culture permeated with drugs, deprivation,
violence, and still managing to make some sort of a life for
themselves and to find some hope. The book is very funny
and at the same time heartbreakingly sad,
but above all it is absolutely accurate.'

Sr Stanislaus Kennedy,
President, Focus Ireland

'This is a hard-hitting novel dealing with a situation which is
becoming increasingly common among young people today.'

Northern People

'*Breaking the Wishbone* is the novel as documentary ... it does
[no]t seem like a novel at all: the result is a venture of high
risk, but one that succeeds magnificently.'

[Th]e *Irish Times*

SIOBHÁN PARKINSON

Siobhán lives in Dublin with her woodturner husband Roger Bennett, and her schoolgoing son Matthew. She is writer-in-residence with Dublin Corporation and the Irish Writers' Centre (1999-2000).

Her previous books include *Amelia, No Peace for Amelia* and *The Leprechaun Who Wished He Wasn't*. Three of her books have been recent Bisto awardwinners: *Four Kids, Three Cats, Two Cows, One Witch (maybe)* won a Bisto Merit Award, *Sisters ... No Way!* won the Bisto Book of the Year Award, and *The Moon King* won a Bisto Merit Award also. *Breaking the Wishbone* is Siobhán's first novel for young adults.

Breaking the Wishbone

A Novel for Young Adults

SIOBHÁN PARKINSON

THE O'BRIEN PRESS
DUBLIN

First published 1999 by The O'Brien Press Ltd,
20 Victoria Road, Dublin 6, Ireland.
Tel. +353 1 4923333; Fax. +353 1 4922777
email: books@obrien.ie
website: www.obrien.ie
Reprinted 1999

ISBN: 0-86278-635-5

British Library Cataloguing-in-publication Data
Parkinson, Siobhan
__ Breaking the wishbone
1.Squatters - Ireland - Dublin - Fiction 2.Alienation (Social
psychology) - Fiction 3.Dublin (Ireland) - Social conditions -
20th century - Fiction 4.Young adult fiction
I.Title
823.9'14[J]

2 3 4 5 6 7 8 9 10
99 00 01 02 03 04 05 06 07

The O'Brien Press receives
assistance from

The Arts Council
An Chomhairle Ealaíon

Layout and design: The O'Brien Press Ltd.
Colour separations: C&A Print Services Ltd.
Printing: Cox & Wyman Ltd.

AUTHOR'S NOTE

The characters in this book are entirely fictitious and bear no resemblance to anyone I have ever known, met or read about. Any resemblance between this story and the experiences of real people is coincidental.

However, although the characters and events are fictitious, they are fairly typical of the experience of young people who live rough, and many of the details in the story are authentic; I am grateful for them to people I met during my years working with Focus Ireland, an organisation that works with people experiencing homelessness.

I am especially grateful to Joe Lucey, whose inspired account of a party held by a group of homeless youngsters in a squat was the initial sparking point for this story. Special thanks to Stanislaus Kennedy, Jean Quinn, Jessica Maybury, Matthew Parkinson Bennett and Roger Bennett for reading and commenting on the manuscript.

To Annette, Karen and Yvonne, with love and thanks
And with very special love also to Nicola

CONTENTS

Prologue page 9

PART ONE

the house that everyone forgot 11

PART TWO

johnner's party 68

PART THREE

from peril and from woe 91

PART FOUR

singing in the rain 137

PART FIVE

a pig in shit 180

PROLOGUE

Picture this. A group of youngsters with nowhere to go, nothing much to do, making the best shift they can in the circumstances.

See it as a documentary, if you like, heads to camera, as they piece together their stories, how they got here, why they left, where they were before, what's happening for them now, where they hope they're going.

You don't have to see it my way, of course. You can see it any way you like – reader's prerogative. Anyway, see what you make of it.

PART 1

the house that
everyone forgot

FADE IN

EXTERIOR: RUNDOWN CITY STREET, DAMP
AFTER RAIN – EVENING

Music: 'Everybody Hurts' by REM

Some of the houses (Georgian? Early Victorian
perhaps?) are derelict, no sign of life, except a
stray dog, nosing in the gutter. Then we see a
young boy, thinly dressed in Manchester United
top and old jeans, crouched on the wet pavement,
his head partially hidden by the collar of his
jersey, which he has drawn up around his face. He
has an aerosol can to his nose and he is sniffing
deeply. HOLD for a BEAT, then PULL BACK INTO –

INTERIOR: SEMI-DERELICT HOUSE – EVENING

The same young boy, dressed as before, is poking
about among his possessions – a sleeping bag,
some clothes. Then he turns to face the camera
and we see him CLOSE-UP and he starts to speak TO
CAMERA.

Johnner

They said it was daft to hold a party in a gaff like ours. It's not really a gaff at all, mind you, not what you would call a place, like. Well, it is a place, I suppose, I mean, it's here, it's probably even got an address, like, officially anyway, though post never gets delivered. I dunno who owns it. I suppose somebody must, like, there must be a register or something, somewhere, where it says who owns which buildings.

Or maybe there isn't. Maybe nobody knows. It's abandoned – so maybe, like, it's been forgotten too. Hey, cool idea. Maybe it's the House that Everyone Forgot. Hey, weee-iird. We're the Kids that Got Away, and we live in the Forgotten House, Beyond the Edge, Derelictionville, Outer Darkness. Hee-eey! Yeah! That's us!

[PAUSE]

Oh, yeah, the party. I was going to tell you about the party – my party. They said you need 'the basics' if you're going to have a party. The basics, according to them – my, eh, flatmates, I suppose you'd call them – well, the basics are electricity, running water and a roof that, like, keeps at least most of the rain out. Not at all, I said, no way. You just need a few mates, a bit of imagination and a lot of crack – not the drug, ha-ha, the fun kind of crack. Well, yeah.

Mind you, you need a few other things as well, I suppose. I have, like, thirteen and a half smokes that I saved up, and two six-packs of beer that Caro, like, liberated from somewhere, plus forty-eight candles behind the curtain.

Ha! You didn't think we had curtains, did you? Well, we have just the one, yeah. Not one pair, one curtain, like, half a pair, I mean, but it's huge and it's nearly big enough to cover the whole window in the bedroom. That's what we call it, the bedroom, even though it's downstairs. It's probably really supposed to be the sittingroom, or maybe you would call it, like, the parlour, in a posh place like this, used to be posh, I mean. It's not so posh now, with, like, the rain coming in and everything, and it's even worse since we got hold of it, but I try to make it nice, yeah.

I put up all my Manchester United posters – yeah! – my old Busby Babes one that my uncle Ken gave me, that's an antique that is, dead cool, and my Cantona-the-King one and my brand new 1999 one with Our Very Own Roy Keane scowling away in the front row. That sickened Beano, it really did, he supports *Liver*pool, like (can you believe it!), but I think he just says that to annoy me, like. I mean, football might as well be something played on another planet for all the interest he takes in it really. Hey, imagine all them aliens with six legs playing football! Feetball they'd have to call it. Hey, yeah!

Anyway, I was saying about the curtain. It's a, well, I mean, *sitting*room sort of curtain, that thick soft stuff, velvet, only with, like, a pattern, sort of flowers on it. The flowers are the same colour as the rest of the curtain, so I don't know if you call that a pattern or not, but anyway, you get the picture. Big, fat, rich sort of curtains, I mean, curtain.

Well, they have a point, like, the rest of them. I'll give them that, up to a point, about the party, I mean. If the weather is really manky, like, then there's definitely a problem. I mean, the rain pours in. Half the slates are off, and they're not all off in the same place, if you see what I mean. I mean, it's not as though there's one big hole to avoid, like, and it's fairly well covered elsewhere. That'd be okay, like. But it's more a sort of a half-made jigsaw puzzle. I mean, there's bits missing all over the shop, and you can get really soaked if you don't dress for the weather, yeah.

We have these really great, like, capes that Beano nicked out of a bicycle shop and we put them on and put the hoods up and we look like bleedin' *pixies*, all sitting around with the water lashing down on us, great gas it is, you should see us, yeah.

We have, like, these plastic bags as well, to put over our sleeping bags. We've built up layers of them, yeah, by this stage, but it still gets in and I mean you can wake up with all these, like, little puddles under your shoulder or around your toes.

But it's not too bad. We sleep downstairs, because then we have the ceiling, like, as well as the roof, I mean, between us and the rain. The ceiling leaks like mad too, but at least it stops some of it, yeah well, maybe not much. I bet one day it's all going to come crumbling down on top of us and kill us, yeah. What a way to go, conked out by a lump of ceiling plaster – yeah! But so long as the weather holds off, like, everything is cool.

I do love living here, I do. It's like camping, I mean, it's like being on your holidays all the time. And nobody wrecks your head here. There's, like, nobody to tell you what to do, ask where you're going, who you're going with, when you'll be back, will you do this, do that, did you do this, did you do that, why did you, why didn't you …

The other stuff we can manage without. Running water, I said, who says we haven't got running water? It's running all *over* the bleedin' place, down the walls, through the roof – cracks me up, that joke about running water, it does – and as for electricity, well sure everyone knows electricity and water don't mix, like, so don't be annoyin' me. That's when I had the brilliant idea. Candles! I do love candles, I do. Add a bit of atmosphere, like. I'm all for atmosphere, I am.

I used to love it when I was real small and we'd have, like, a power cut at home. My ma would get out the candles. She always kept, like, a box of them under the sink, and there'd be four or five in it, some of them just, like, stubs. She'd light one candle, yeah, and then she'd soften the bottom of another one, like, in the flame, until the wax began to run, and then she'd fix the candle on a saucer, sort of, you know, anchoring it in its own grease. She'd light that candle next, and so on until they were all lit and set on their saucers, and then she'd put them around the place, and they'd flicker away and, like, *sparkle* and the flat would look completely different, sort of, like, magical, like oh, Fairyland or somewhere, yeah. I know that's stupid. I mean, I know what people would say if I started talking about bleedin' *Fairy*land. But it was like that, really it was, yeah. You couldn't, like, see all the mess everywhere, just these little flames and around them there'd be, like, these pools of half-light, all hazy at the edges, and things that were near the candles would *glow* and you'd see the flames the way they'd be reflected in things like the teapot or the mirror, yeah.

I used to love that, I did, the way we'd all just sit there, just *gazing* at the candlelight. My ma used to make us sit real quiet, because she has a horror, like, of fire. That's because of my auntie Greta, who was her little sister, like, getting badly burnt as a baby. She was terrified, I mean, that if we went bollocking around as usual we'd knock the candles over and start a bleedin' fire, so she made us sit real still, and I remember that we used to talk, like, in whispers. I don't know whether the smell of candlewax made us think of churches or wha', or whether it was just the candlelight, I mean the way it was, like, all soft and glowy, but anyway we'd sit there and watch these big sort of shadows, and they would be jerking away across the bleedin' *ceiling*, like. It was weird not being able to watch telly or make tea or do *any*thing, yeah. I remember once my mother said, oh well, I may as well get a bit of ironing done, seeing as I can't do anything else, and none of us realised until she went to plug the iron in and then, I mean, we all got it at the same *time*, like, and we all burst out laughing together. That was nice, real nice, us all together and everyone just *laughing* at how stupid we all were, yeah.

It wasn't because of my ma that I left, I mean, *she* wasn't the one that gave me grief. It's my da doesn't like me. I don't really know why, I never done nothing on him, I think I just get up his nose, you know that way? It's the same with my brothers, yeah. He never got on with the boys. The girls, like, didn't have problems with him, or not much, but he was always picking on us.

All you had to do was have, like, an *opinion*. It didn't have to be an opinion about him, even, or anything to do with him, but as soon as you said what you thought about anything at all, I mean, he'd be all over you, a fist under your nose, and his breath would be, like, in your face, and it would be hot and stinking of beer, I mean, absolutely rancid, I swear.

I don't know why. I never really understood it. My ma said he was beat up by *his* da, and that was what made him like that, but I dunno, I mean, *I* don't beat people up, do I? Well, I mean, I don't. It was worse even than when we were small. Then he used to beat us, like, black and blue, but then it'd be over. But, I mean, this roughing up and threatening is worse, because it all rumbles away and never really comes to a head, like, and so, I mean, you're always tiptoeing around trying not to get him going, like. In the end it got too much for me. I had to get out, yeah, I just couldn't hack it any more.

But anyway, remembering that about the smell of the candles and us all whispering and everything, well, that gave me the idea for the candles. Church, I thought, that's where you get candles. They have them there for, like, the shrines, in these sort of big brass drawers with no fronts. That's where I robbed them out of.

There's, like, a slot for the money. You're supposed to put the money in the slot and then light a candle, ten pence a shot. I had a ten-pee piece in my pocket, so I put it in the slot. I mean, I don't like robbing out of churches. It's not that I believe in all that stuff, I mean, I'm not expecting God to suddenly let a roar out of him and strike me down or nothing, but it just doesn't seem right, I mean, so that's why I put in the ten pence.

It's not God so much, it's more people like my nana, I mean, she's really into churches and praying and stuff, I don't like to do anything that would upset her, even though she hadn't a clue about the candles. I suppose I sort of felt that the ten pence made it, like, nearly all right, I mean, especially as those half-arsed little candles aren't worth that much.

Anyway, I put my ten pence in the slot, like, and I threw in a few coppers I had as well, for good measure, I mean, and then I took as many candles as I could carry, yeah. I stuffed them into all my pockets. Cleared out the shrine to some nun called The Little Flower, I did. Sorry, me old flower, I said to her, but my need is greater than yours, sort of thing. Next time, I'll make it St Anthony, I promised her, you know, even things up, yeah.

So now we have, like, all these candles. They're real scutty little things, them shrine candles, but still, I have loads of them, I have, so they should make a good show. Cool. I must remember to keep some of them back so that we can light a second lot, otherwise it'll all be over in, like, half an hour. Oh, it's going to be gorgeous, I know it is, with all the candles, better than a birthday cake, it'll be all glowing, yeah, and you won't be able to see, like, the state of the place in the candlelight, I mean, just the candles and a load of shadows. I can just imagine it, all lit up like Christmas, all little flickering pools of yellow light like jewels, only, like, *alive*, yeah.

Getting the candles like that really got me going about the party idea. I mean, I began to believe it could really happen, you know, that it was *possible*.

I showed them to the others, I did, the candles, I mean. Mad, they said, and they wanted to light them there and then, all of them. They're all like that, always wanting everything to happen *now*. Not me. I mean, I like planning things and enjoying them, I do, before they happen, that way you get, like, more *value* out of things, but they all want everything to be always happening right now.

I had to fight them off, I did. I said we could light one tonight, but the rest we have to keep, like, for the party. I put one on the table (it's really an upside down, like, tea chest that we found in the basement) and I hid the rest in the bottom of my sleeping bag, in case they nicked them on me. I mean, it's not that they're always taking my stuff or anything, they're good mates, really they are, but they do get carried away sometimes, they do, especially if they have drink taken.

Not that any of us ever has much money for drink. I mean, Beano is eighteen, now, and he's on the labour, I think he must be anyway, because he always seems to have money. Caroline is on some sort of, like, FÁS course, I think she is anyway, because she's flush sometimes too, and Curly, he's on a course as well, only I don't think they give him much, and Samantha and me, we're always, I mean *always*, skint.

My sister gives me money, though, sometimes. She has two kids and another one on the way, so she hasn't much to spare, like, but sometimes when she gets her money she does give me a few bob for myself, especially if I've been doing, like, a few jobs for her. I mean, I help her out sometimes, like, take the clothes to the launderette, maybe, or keep an eye on the kids for her, like, if she has to go out.

She wanted me to move in with her when I left my ma's because, I mean, her fella's inside and she gets lonely sometimes with only the kids for company, yeah, and the social workers are always on her back, turning up and asking questions about the kids, especially if they have any sort of, like, a cut or a bruise at all, it drives her mad, it does, as if kids aren't always falling over and doing something to themselves. It's all because of Damien, it is. It makes them, like, suspicious, him having a record, I mean. She's afraid some day she's going to hit one of them (one of the social workers, I mean, not the kids, she'd never hit the kids, she's mad about them, she is). If she does that, hits one I mean, she'll really be in trouble. She used to do a bit of karate, like, and she could kick you into the middle of next week if she really got going, yeah.

She thought maybe if I was there she could, like, cope

better with it, so we gave it a try for a while, but it didn't work out, I mean, we fought all the time. She treated me like one of the kids, she did, she used to, like, forget sometimes I wasn't one of hers. But when I moved here, got a bit of independence, like, that all changed. She's glad to see me now when I go round to her place, she is, appreciates my help. Yeah, right, she said when I told her that, and gave me an elbow in the ribs.

But she's okay, is Lorraine. I mean, sometimes she gives me cigarettes if she hasn't got any readies. I don't smoke. I used to get these, like, terrible chest infections when I was a kid, really terrible they were. In Temple Street twice I was, with pneumonia. I'm fine now, but it put me off anything that makes me cough, like, and smoking makes me cough, or it did the couple of times I tried it, so I don't.

People sometimes treat you like a right wimp if you don't smoke, but I mean, what's the point if it makes you sick, and anyway I can't afford it. My ma smokes forty a day, she does, and she says she's a martyr to them. But it's handy to have a few smokes on you all the same. I mean, it's amazing the things you can get people to do for you if they are, like, desperate for a smoke. And it's nice to have something to give people, sort of make, like, a contribution, especially if you're like me and always short of cash.

That reminds me, I must see if I can get a few more smokes for this party. Can't have a party with that lot without smokes, no way. They should have their own, of course, but they're always running out of fags, they are.

They buy a package of ten, and they smoke, like, five right off and then the other five over the next few hours, and then they're back where they started. I can't understand that. I mean, like I say, I don't smoke, so I suppose I don't really understand it all anyway, like, but if I had, say, a bar of chocolate or a package of them Mikado – I do love Mikado, I do – I'd only have one square, like, or one biscuit and then I'd keep the rest for another time. I mean, I get more value out of things than they do, but they just laugh at me about that.

'Lighten up, Johnner,' Beano is always saying. 'Seize the day.' I don't know what that means. I mean, I know what 'lighten up' means – I hate that expression, my da was always telling me to lighten up – but 'seize the day' is, like, something I really can't make head or tail of, no way can I work it out. A day isn't something you can seize, is it? I used to think it was 'cease the day', but Lorraino put me right on that. Still doesn't make any sense, though.

Drink is the other thing you have to have for a party, but I don't know where I'm going to get that, apart from the two six-packs Caroline gave me. I mean, well, she didn't exactly *give* them to me. She came belting in one day, like, with one under each arm and I was the only person here. She half flung them at me, and she said, 'There y'are, Johnner, hide them, willya, I don't want Beano gettin' them.'

Caroline is gorgeous. Samantha is real nice too. I mean, she thinks she's looking after me, you know, as if I was, like, a kid or something. She's nice looking too, I think, her hair is nice, all curly and bouncy, and she has a nice friendly face, yeah. Caroline, now, is not as friendly to me as Samantha, sometimes I think she's sort of sad in herself, like, she doesn't talk much, but she's beautiful, yeah. She's dead tall and thin and she wears these, like, short skirts, real tight, they look as if they've *grown* on her body, and when she gets dressed up in the evening and puts that glittery stuff on her face, she looks like a film star, yeah.

So anyway, I hid the beer, and then I think she must have forgotten about the cans, because, I mean, she didn't ask me again where they were. That's what gave me the idea about this party in the first place, like, I mean it's not often we have two six packs between the five of us.

Still, it's not enough for, like, a party. I have to get some more, somehow. First I have to think about paying for it, and then, I mean, I have to think about actually, like, *getting* it. I'm too young to buy it, and anyway I'm small for my age, so they never give it to me in the bleedin' supermarket. I suppose Beano could get it, but he's just as likely to do a runner with the money. Ah no, he's not, I'm only messing. But still, I wish I could get it myself. This over-eighteen lark is a load of cowshite. I mean, it's enough to make you want to puke, isn't it? As if when you turn eighteen, like, you're suddenly some sort of, oh, I don't know, model citizen or something, responsible enough to be able to go to dirty movies and buy beer. But I mean, why would a model citizen *want* to go to dirty movies? It doesn't make any sense at all, no more than seize the day.

Anyway, I'll worry about buying the beer when I work out how to get the money. I suppose I could knock it off, but I'm not good at that. I mean, I always look suspicious, for one thing, but the other thing is, I feel, like, bad for the shopkeeper, yeah. I have this terrible habit of seeing things from, like, other people's point of view. It's an awful handicap in life. I mean, I keep thinking the shopkeeper has had to pay for the beer, like, and it's not fair if I take it off him. Sometimes, I think it would be nice to be able to do a sort of deal with the shopkeeper: say, 'Oi, I won't nick these things if you'll give them to me for what you paid for them. That way, you don't lose out and I get the beer dead cheap. Okay?'

God, imagine if I told the rest of them that? They would, like, break their sides laughing at that idea. I mean, they're good mates and all, but they have, like, a funny sense of humour sometimes. You have to be careful what you say or they'd be bursting themselves at you, they would.

I like beer I do, we all do, but cider is cheaper, more bang for your buck, know what I mean? Maybe the couple of six-packs would be enough and we could, like, stretch it with a few cans of apple. That's my ma talking now. She's forever stretching things with other things. Stretching the mince with bleedin' breadcrumbs, yeah, stretching the dinner with spuds, stretching the butter with marge, stretching the batch loaf by slicing it up real thin, which is very hard to do, I'll have you know, massive crumbs a batch loaf makes if you try cutting it too thin. Poor oul' Ma. I do miss her. I should go up to see her more often, but the oul' fella is nearly always around.

I went to see Ma after I left Lorraine's place. I didn't know where I was going to go. I thought I'd see Ma and ask if she had any, like, ideas. I suppose I kind of half thought I might go back home, I mean, just for a while, just till I got my act together, like, got myself settled a bit, but as soon as I set a foot inside that door, I knew I couldn't do it. He was there, sitting in his oul' chair, reading the *Star*, and sniping away at me the minute I opened my mouth, needling me. God, he really does my head in. He doesn't have to raise a bleedin' hand to me. It's enough for him to open his mouth and I want to go for him, mash his face in. Not that I would. I mean, I wouldn't have the nerve. He's much stronger than me anyway. I'm, like, dead skinny. Weedy, I suppose you would say, though my ma says I'll 'fill out', whatever that's supposed to mean. He's the opposite, short and thick and sort of *compressed*, you know, like a bottle of Calor gas, all that power packed down real tight into a barrel shape. Makes me feel nearly squashed and breathless even *thinking* about him, as if he had given me a belt in the stomach that plastered me up against the wall, yeah.

Hey, I shouldn't be even thinking about him, I shouldn't. Can't do nothing about him anyhow, and he's not a problem in my life now. I have *no* problems since I got shacked up here. It's great, it is, yeah. Great to have your own place and all, where you can be with your own mates, and they're all great mates, I mean great fun,

dead nice. And we are going to have one almighty party!
Yee-ha!

I do *love* it here. I really do. Just love it. It's freedom it
is, living here, freedom and peace.

[CUT TO –]

Young girl, curly-haired and good-natured looking,
dressed in a tracksuit, hunched against the cold,
on a broken-down sofa, and chafing one shoeless
foot, as if trying to warm it.

Samantha

I hate this dump, so I do. It's so *cold*. Sometimes you'd
swear the walls were actually *radiating* cold, you know,
the way a radiator radiates heat, only it's cold. And it's
damp, so it is. No, I tell a lie. It's not damp. It's *wet*, it's
sopping, it's dripping, that's the long and the short of it.
Every surface you touch is clammy. Mind you, sometimes you touch something and, I swear to God, it's so
cold you can't tell whether it really is damp or just so cold
that it *feels* damp. The walls, well you can expect them to
be cold, the doors, the windows, the floors, all the hard
surfaces, but even your clothes feel cold when you touch
them, as if they have been in the fridge, even the clothes
you are wearing, the top layer anyway. You go to pick up
a towel or a dishcloth, and I swear to God it's like hand-
ling a dead fish.

And everything smells. The kitchen is a health hazard,
that's the long and the short of it. Your feet stick to the

floor when you walk on it, and they go on sticking for a while after you come out of it. Whatever is on the floor there must get on your shoes and then you carry it around the house, I suppose.

There's a sink in the kitchen – which is how you know it's the kitchen. It's one of them old cracked cream ones, so it is, only it's all stained brown. It has taps, but there's no water. The house three doors up has a tap at the back, for watering the garden I suppose, and it works, so we get our water from there. We climb over the wall with buckets, after it gets dark, and fill them up, so we do. That's a bit of gas sometimes, clanking around with buckets in the dark. Someone lives there, an old man, I think. He must know we do it, but fair play to him, he leaves us alone, doesn't want trouble, I suppose.

Of course no water means no jacks either. We pee out the back, when it's dark – though, mind you, the boys pee out there even when it's daytime, but that's blokes for you, no shame. I hate the way they do that. Girls have more self-respect, I think.

For the *other* we have to make what you might call alternative arrangements. There is a public toilet about a mile away, so there is, but it is a stinking hell-hole, and that's a fact. I was in it once and I swear to God I wouldn't go near it again – not if I had dysentery, I wouldn't.

What I usually do is I find a pub or a shop or a café or somewhere that has a 'Ladies', so I do. There's plenty of those, but of course they are supposed to be for customers only, so you have to sneak past the barman or whoever. And then again, you can't keep going back to the same places, because they'd get to recognise you, so they would.

You have to keep yourself looking presentable too, or you wouldn't be let in. I like to keep clean anyway. I swear to God, I'd hate to be one of them homeless-looking people with crusty heads and the soles flapping off their shoes. But then again, it's not easy, that, when you have no running water. It takes forever to boil up enough for a cup of tea on that camping-gas thing we have, so it does, not to mind trying to get enough to wash your hair in.

There is this sort of centre, for kids that haven't got a place. It's sort of like a huge garage or a warehouse, but then again it has these couches and pool tables and stuff in it, and it has these mad spray-paintings on the walls that are meant to make you feel at home, I think, and fair play to them, they let you have a shower and all, so they do. They want you to do art and stuff and they try to talk to you about FÁS courses – God, can you imagine *me* on a FÁS course? But then again, I just have the shower and a cup of tea if it's going, and I smile a lot at the fella that's in charge and take the leaflets. That's how I manage, anyway, I swear to God. I go there twice a week to get cleaned up and I get by on a quick lick with cold water and a lot of deodorant the rest of the time, so I do.

They even have a hairdryer. I never had a hairdryer. It's mad when you think about it, I mean, they only cost a few pounds, but then again, because it's electric, you sort of think it's like a telly or a microwave or something real dear that you could never afford, unless you nicked it, I suppose.

Hairdryers are great, so they are, because you're feeling all cold after your shower, and you can run the hot air all over yourself and warm up, before you dry your hair. When I get out of here and get a proper place to live, I swear to God I am going to have hairdryers in every room, and any time I am feeling a bit cold, I can just turn it on and stick it up my jumper for a minute, or even take off my shoes and spray lovely hot air on my toes. Warm feet is my idea of heaven, so it is. Then again, warm all *over* is my idea of heaven, but warm feet is definitely the most important thing.

I'm never warm here, so I amn't. Curly, fair play to him, he gave me this stupid hot-water bottle. I do use it sometimes, but we only have a saucepan to boil water in, and it's hard to pour the hot water out of a saucepan into a hot-water bottle, so it is. I'm terrified I'm going to scald myself. All the same, I thought it was dead-on of him to think of the hot-water bottle. He is very sweet, Curly, fair play to him, even though he looks as if he would slice up his grandmother and have her on toast for breakfast. I swear to God it's all an act, the boots and the sleeveless jerkin and the tattoos and the pierced eyebrow and the shaved head and everything. He says he does it to look tough, because he knows he's not. If he dressed in jeans and a jumper, people would just walk on him, he says.

He wears combat trousers, and he is really pissed off that everyone wears combats now. It used to be just people like him that wore all the gear, but now you see *girls* wearing them, he says, and I swear to God, he says 'girls' as if was a dirty word. Kids who go to posh schools and get collected by their mummies in shiny little purple or lemon-coloured cars, you know, like Skittles on wheels, they wear them, so they do. That really depresses Curly and especially them black-and-white ones. Combats are supposed to be *khaki*, he says, or in that brown-and-khaki-leaves camouflage pattern. What's the point of a camouflage pattern in black and white? You might be camouflaged in a herd of pandas, but then again, what is the point of that if you live in the inner city?

I think it's kind of funny that he lets it get to him so much, I mean, when you think about the things we have to cope with, but then again I wouldn't dream of laughing at him, so I wouldn't. He's very sensitive, though you wouldn't think it to look at him – except for his ears. I think his ears give it away. I swear to God he has the smallest ears I have ever seen on a fella. Much smaller than mine. They look sort of apologetic, I swear to God, as if they think they shouldn't be there at all. That's really what Curly is like – sorry to be taking up oxygen, wishing he could breathe less so he wouldn't be using up the air on the rest of us. I like that about him, he's not a bit pushy, like a lot of fellas is.

Beano, now, is the exact opposite. He dresses dead smart, mostly in black, and he gels his hair and all and swoops it back off his face, which is sort of bony and pale and I suppose quite handsome. Curly is not handsome, it has to be said. His hair is the wrong shade of red, the shade that clashes with everything, and his face is kind of soft and squidgy-looking and his skin is piggy-pink – it's so pink you can't tell where his lips begin and end – and he's still a bit pimply, though mainly it's acne scars around his jawbones. Even his eyes are the wrong colour, I swear to God, too pale, but then again they are very far apart, which gives him a sort of surprised look that's kind of nice in a dreamy sort of way. I think so anyway. I think he has a nice expression, even if he's not good-looking.

I swear to God, that Beano looks like someone that works in the films, so he does, or maybe as a roadie with a rock band or something dead cool anyway. He should wear shades really, they would suit the look, so they would. But then again, he gives me the creeps. I always think he's *leering* at me. I swear to God it makes me feel naked. I don't know how Caro puts up with him. I think she's scared of him, so I do.

I don't mind the robbing and that. You have to rob to live, so you do. It's not that. It's not even the gear either, though I don't like that. I mean, in fairness, I don't mind the odd joint, like Curly does, and I've done E a few times myself, though I know it's a bit risky because, when it comes down to it, you never know what's going to be in it, do you? But gear is different, so it is. Once you're into that, your soul is not your own any more, that's what I think anyway. I know there's people says it's all propaganda, that it's not that addictive *really*, but I swear to God, I look at what I see around me and I know what I know. You'll do anything for a hit, you will, once you're hooked, and I mean *anything*, you'd smother your mother for it, so you would. (I'd smother my mother anyway, if I got half a chance, fat lot of good as a mother she was, and that's the long and the short of it, but that's another story.)

Still, though, in fairness, it's not the gear that bothers me about Beano. That's his problem, is the way I look at it. It's just *him* I don't like, and that's a fact. There's something about him, and the way he treats Caroline that makes me mad, so there is. She's a lovely girl, is Caroline, and he just treats her like a piece of shit, so he does. I keep telling Curly, but Curly, poor oul' Curly, he's such a big softie, he just says, yeah, Sam, he's a bad lot, you're right there, and he goes on doing absolutely nothing about getting us out of here. Sometimes, I swear to God, I could shake him.

If we're going to get out of here, it has to be me that makes the move, no two ways about it. That's one thing about the way I grew up, you learn fast enough how to watch out for yourself. When you're one of a bunch of kids in a children's home, it's every man for himself, so it is. But the thing is, I have to think of Johnner, too. I can't just up and leave with Curly and abandon that kid, so I can't. Beano would eat him without salt and spit out his bones if there was no one around to protect him, the poor little scrap, and that's the long and the short of it.

You couldn't help but like him, Johnner, I mean, he's that daft and dreamy and trusting. I mean, look how he just came along with me, I mean, I could've been a spy for a paedophile ring or a child pornography racket or *any*thing, you know, I mean, there's all sorts of sleazy types out there, so there is, worse than Beano even, picking up likely young fellas off the street. Mind you, I think now in fairness he must've been on something that day, Johnner, probably glue or something, because he was out of it, completely out of it he was. The roaring out of him! He was sitting on the street and roaring at the people passing, so he was. I was going past, and says I to myself, that young fella's going to get himself arrested, the stupid eejit, why doesn't he shut up, but then again I looked at him sitting there in the drizzly rain on the footpath, so I did, it was all wet and it was getting to be night-time, and his trousers was all soaked, and I swear to God, it went to my heart to see him. Oh God, says I to myself, I can't leave him here, he should be at home with his mammy, so he should, he's only a kid.

So I get talking to him and says I to him, he could come back to our place for the night, but he had to stop shouting. His mouth was hanging open, and his eyes was glazed over, and I didn't think he was really listening to me, but fair play to him, the next thing he gives a little nod, and then he smiles at me. A sort of a crooked smile, and I swear to God it broke my heart the way he looked at me, all in bits he was, but he still smiled, so he did. He's too young for this sort of life, says I to myself, I can't leave him here on the street.

Well, see, I was remembering, thinking back to the day I met Caro and how *she* helped *me* out, so, anyway, I just put out my hand to him, so I did, and I pulled him up, and I half-carried him back to the squat.

One thing about him, young Johnner, he's good for a laugh, so he is. I mean, half of you would want to give him a good shake and tell him to get a grip, the other half of you would feel for sorry for the poor little shite, and another half again would just bust your ass laughing at him. That's three halves, but you know what I mean. Thirds, I suppose I should say.

Fair play to him, he bounced back pretty quick, when you think of the state he was in the night I met him. He's like a four-year-old now, all shiny-eyed about this oul' party he wants to have. I mean, I swear to God we're only half in it, the lot of us, it's as much as we can do to get from one end of the week to the other – what am I saying? From one end of the *day* to the other more like – but there's oul' Johnner planning a feckin' *party*. But you know, there's something about him that would get around you, so there is, and before you know it, you find yourself offering to make fairy cakes.

No, of course I didn't offer to make fairy cakes, that was my idea of a little joke. I didn't offer to blow up balloons either, so I didn't. But I did find myself agreeing that a party was a great idea and asking him who he wanted to invite. That was when I felt sorry for him. He has these big soppy eyes, too big for his face nearly, they look, and they were all shining and excited-looking when he was talking about his party, so they were, but when I asked him who he wanted to invite, he looked away. He muttered something: 'Lorraino, I suppose.' I think that's the sister's name, it must be, I think. Then I realised that it's all in his head really, so it is, all this excitement. He hasn't got a big pile of friends bursting to let their hair down, so he hasn't. It's all just an *idea* he has. Poor little sod, he just wants to have a good time, but he hasn't a clue how to go about it, so he hasn't. So anyway, I ended up by saying I'd help him with the party, so now I've promised, I'll have to do something about it.

He showed me his little collection of treasures – a few scutty oul' candles, a bunch of half-battered, stale-looking smokes and two six-packs of Guinness. 'That's great, Johnner,' says I. 'You have the makings of a right party there.' And then I made my mistake. 'I'll see if I can get you a few cans,' I said.

So now I have to find some cans for this eejity party. But sure, I suppose I'll be able to manage something. I know he can't buy drink, because he's way under age. I am too, though not as young as him of course, but I look older, especially if I put on my lipstick and change out of my Tear-aways, which is what I usually wear, and put on a skirt. I have a skirt somewhere, I think, but I haven't got any tights, and it would freeze the bum off you going around in high heels with a short skirt and no tights, and that's a fact.

But what do you think happened this morning? I woke up early as usual, about nine o'clock, which is plenty early enough if you've nowhere to go for the day, so it is. I was doing my usual thing of staying in the sleeping bag for as long as possible, because it's the only place I'm warm. At least, I'm warm in it in the morning when I wake up, apart from my feet, which are *permanently* cold, I swear to God, since we came to this feckin' place, so I hardly count those any more when I'm thinking about warm and cold.

So where was I? Oh yes, well, as I say, it's funny how you're warm when you wake up, isn't it, so even if your nose is cold, which mine usually is, because you can't keep your nose inside the sleeping bag, so you can't, not if you want to survive the night, and even if your feet are cold, which mine always are, because I think they've sort of become permanently deep-frozen like two Christmas turkeys from Dunnes stuck on the end of your legs, so when you wake up, the last thing you want to do is get up, because then you lose that lovely warmy feeling that lasts about half an hour after you wake. (God, I can't stop thinking about the cold. It's the thing that gets to me most about living here, so it is.)

So anyway, this morning, there I was enjoying my morning warm-in, which I try to spin out as long as possible, but I always end up overdoing it, so I do, and then I start to get chilled to the bone lying there and then I just have to get up to get the circulation going again or I will die of exposure, no two ways about it, when suddenly something comes flying through the air at me and lands on my face, I swear to God, real soft, nearly like someone touching you. I put out my hand from inside the sleeping bag, so I did, and I felt whatever it was. It was all soft and silky to touch, but it was cold – so what's new? – like everything else around here, I swear to God. I brought out my other hand so I could hold whatever it was up in front of my face and take a proper look at it. And wasn't it a tiny little micro-mini-skirt, and it was made of some sort of velvety material, very slinky, though, slinkier than you'd expect velvet to be, and pure black like the night.

Then comes Caroline's voice: 'Keep it if you want it,' she says.

'Hey Caro, that's your best skirt, the one you wear for going out in,' says I. 'You can't give it away.'

'I can't wear it,' Caro said, but she wouldn't explain any more, and the next thing, I swear to God, a pair of tights came flying through the air as well, a black pair, dead sheer, and with only a little rip at the toe, no actual ladders or nothing – I know because I checked later, so I did.

'You might as well have them too,' says she, and – I know this sounds soft but I can't explain it any other way – her voice sounded sort of *empty*. 'They go with the skirt,' says she.

'What about you, Caroline?' I asked her then. 'Do you not want to wear this any more? Is it after going out of style or what?' I couldn't believe she was giving stuff away, you know.

I thought she might have got mad at me then for saying that, so I did, but she only shrugged and she turned over in her own sleeping bag, and then she says in a real muffled voice, 'Take them or leave them, Sam, but stop going *on* about them, okay?'

Well, anyway, I took them, so I did, sure what else would I do? I got up and I tried on the skirt. It looked a bit stupid over my tracksuit bottoms, I have to say, but I was too cold to take them off, so I was. Later, says I to myself, when I get a bit of heat into me. So then I put on my runners and I went into the kitchen to boil up some water to make tea and warm my feet.

Not the *same* water, of course. I make the tea *first*, and while it's drawing I put on a second saucepan and when that's warmed up a bit I throw it into a basin and stick my feet in it to thaw them out. That's my favourite moment of the whole day, I swear to God, putting my feet in warm water in the morning, soaking up the warmth. I swear, I'm like an oul' one the way I do be going on about the cold, but it gets right into you, you know, so that you can't think of anything else, not even the hunger, and that's a fact.

So anyway, once the feet were nice and pinky from the hot water (wiggle, wiggle, howya toes, nice and warm, huh?) and when I had them dried on an old T-shirt I keep for a towel, and after I had a good hot cup of tea inside me and another one poured, mainly for keeping my hands warm, I thought I might chance trying on my new outfit, so I stripped off the tracksuit and slipped into the tights. I threw my tracksuit bottoms on the floor, so I did, and I stood on them, like a mat, so I wouldn't have to touch the manky oul' cold floor with my nice warm barely-black feet and I did a little twirl, twisting to admire myself all around. God, I was gorgeous, I could see that even without a mirror. I thought you had to have legs that go on forever, so I did, to look as good as Caroline in a dead short skirt, but really, as long as they're not *awful* dumpy or fat or hairy or anything, *anyone's* legs can look good in the right tights, and that's a fact.

The next thing there came a wolf-whistle, whi-whi-eeew. I swear to God, I hate that kind of a whistle, so I do. It makes me jump, and anyway I always think it sounds sort of sarky, as if the person doing it is really sending you up instead of admiring you, which is what he's pretending to be doing. It was Beano, so it was, and he was slouching against the door jamb.

'Jay, you're lookin' great this mornin', Samantha,' he said, all smarmy-like. 'You have a great pair of legs on you.'

I suppose it was meant to come across as a compliment, but it I swear to God, it sounded like something you'd say about a racehorse or a greyhound or something. It made me want to tuck my gorgeous legs away somewhere, so it did, but there was nowhere I could put them, and there was no point in pulling the little skirt down towards my knees, it would only draw attention to how short it was. So instead of hiding my legs, I lifted one knee up and gave my ankle a sort of a sexy little twist and I said, 'You like, Mister?' but it was really because I was embarrassed, and that's the long and the short of it, I didn't know what else to say to him. Then I did this sort of a silly pirouette, holding my hands out stiffly, you know, with the fingers all pointing outwards, like a little girl in one of them puffy party dresses.

'I liiiiiike,' says he, and he was looking at me with his eyes half-closed, and raising one eyebrow high above his eye, in a sort of a pointy arc. (I don't know how he does that. I've practised and practised, but all I've ever managed is to wiggle my ears like a stupid bunny rabbit, and that's a fact.)

I threw my head back and I gave one of them little silvery laughs, so I did, God, I blush even thinking about it, the sort girls do in the films when they toss their hair back at fellas. I was just playing a part really, and that's a fact, pretending to be somebody I'm not – and I don't even *want* to be – but for some reason it was the only way I could think of to act with him, so it was. He gave this real low laugh, a sort of a chuckle I suppose you would call it, just like a movie star, I don't think, all cool and smooth and distant.

And then, very suddenly, I swear to God, his smile turned to a snarl and he snapped out: 'Hey, is that Caro's skirt you're wearing? The one I bought for her?' (Bought? I don't think Beano ever bought anything in his life, everything he ever owned since he got too big for his toy trainset he robbed, and that's a fact.)

'Ye-eh,' says I, feeling like I was getting the third degree. I didn't want a row with Beano over a stupid skirt, but I didn't want to start a row between him and Caro either, so I didn't. 'She ga– lent it to me.'

'*Lent* it to you? What'd she do that for? That's her working skirt, I mean, her best skirt for going out in.'

I thought that was a funny thing to say, about her working skirt. But anyway, I said, 'Yeah, well I know that, Beano, but she just lent it to me, okay? Maybe she thought it would suit me?'

'Suit you?' God he's really roaring now, I swear to God. 'What's that got to do with it? Wait till I get my …'

'I tell you what, Beano,' says I suddenly, thinking real quick – that's me all over. 'Would you like a cup of tea? It's fresh in the pot. It'll take the chill out of you, isn't it terrible cold this morning?'

I was jabbering on, so I was, changing the subject, and he knew it, but all of a sudden, just the way he got suddenly nasty, now he turned on the charm again and says he in his cool voice, 'Yeah, well, maybe I will so, darlin'.'

God, I hate anyone calling me darlin'. It makes me feel about a hundred, so it does. So anyway, I poured him a cup of tea without another word, and he took it from me and went off someplace with it.

Now that I had the skirt on, I thought I might as well go and get the booze I promised Johnner, so I finished my tea, rinsed up after myself, splashed cold water on my face, and ran a comb through my hair. I had to clean my teeth with my finger, so I had, and put a stick of chewing gum in my mouth, because I haven't got toothpaste or a toothbrush. So then I picked up my tracksuit trousers, and I tiptoed quickly back into the bedroom to get a pair of decent shoes, I changed my tracksuit top and I put on the least smelly tank-top I could find. Then I slung my CAT bag over my shoulder and … I sashayed off, so I did, out into the world. Dha-dha!

[PAUSE, Music, then CUT TO–]

Well, I had a successful morning, so I had, dead proud of myself, I am. I went around to that little off-licence place around the corner. Well, it's not really around the corner, it's around about three corners, but anyway, I went in to your man there, Bojo. That can't be a real name, but that's what they call him anyway, but I always call him Mr O'Brien, because he likes that, the ould eejit. Anyway, I went in and says I to him, 'Good morning, Mr O'Brien,' and I gave him all this spiel about the weather and everything. Nobody talks to that ould fella, because he's a sour old bastard. So he's all delighted when I come in and start bullshitting him about the weather. It's kind of sad, really, I suppose, but sure what can you do?

It's an off-licence, so it is, but he has all these old-fashioned sweets too, that he sells, cough sweets and bulls' eyes and stuff like that that your granny used to eat, and they're all in big jars up behind the counter, so they are, and I always ask him for lemon bon-bons, because that jar is on the highest shelf and he has to get out this little stepladder thing he has, and you can slip a few things into your bag dead handy while he's getting it all set up. The poor eejit, he's so terrified of getting robbed he has all these glass shelfy-sort of things all over the counter, and they're all piled up with stuff, so he nearly has to stand on his tippy-toes to see out over it all. I think he feels more secure when he has all this stuff in front of him, but it means he can't really see what's going on, so he can't, unless he's standing in one particular spot. He's a harmless sort of a poor bugger really, but then again, he can be a bit of an old sourpuss, so it serves him right, is how I look at it.

Anyway, wasn't I just holding this four-pack of big cans of Heineken, all set to drop it into the bag, when old Bojo turns around on his little stepladder and says he, 'I'm out of the lemon, will the white bon-bons do you?' I nearly dropped my drawers, so I did. But quick as a flash, says I to him, 'God, you know, I was nearly going to buy these cans, only I remembered you have this real strict over-twenty-one policy. Oh, yeah, the white'll do fine, thanks, Mr O'Brien.'

He was dead suspicious, but then again, he likes me, see, so I think he didn't want to be suspicious, the poor ould fart, he was in a bit of a puzzle about what to think, I could see that, so anyway, he got down off his stepladder real slow like, and I could see he was going to ask me to open my bag, so before he could say anything, I clapped my hand across my mouth, so I did, and says I, 'Oh janey, Mr O'Brien, I'm after forgetting my purse. I tell you what, I'll run home for it and I'll be back in a jiff!' And I legged it off out the door, and I could hear him roaring at me to come back.

I think I'll have to give that place a miss for a while, but sure the main thing is I had a good haul anyway. I already had a four-pack of Bulmer's, and two bottles of red wine, Australian I think it was, or South African, or maybe Argentinean, somewhere with an A anyway. I stashed that lot away in a corner of the bedroom, under my half-worn clothes – that's the ones I've worn a few times but are still good for a few more goes before they get to the stage where they have to go to the launderette. (I hate even having to think like that, so I do, but you can't have the high standards you would like when you live like this.)

When I got back, Beano had disappeared, I don't know where Johnner was, Curly was gone off to his course as usual, so it was just me and Caro. She was still all curled up in her sleeping bag, with her back to me.

'Hey Caroline,' says I, and I gives her back a little prod with the toe of my shoe, 'here look at me in your best skirt. What do you think?'

'Would you ever eff off,' said Caroline from inside the sleeping bag.

Caroline never talks like that to me, I swear to God she doesn't, not even if she's hung-over, which she wasn't, so far as I know. It's not like her to be ratty, so it isn't, and it didn't square with giving me the skirt earlier either, so it didn't. Although come to think of it, then again, she *threw* it at me. It wasn't exactly what you would call gift-wrapped and sealed with a loving kiss, now, in fairness. She was behaving sort of weird, I thought, all things considered.

I squatted down to her. She still had her back to me, but I put my hand on her shoulder and says I, 'All right, Caro?'

'Yeah,' she muttered. 'Just lea'me alone.'

'Feeling a bit under the weather?'

She didn't answer, she just lets this long low groan.

'Tea, my girl, that's what you need.' I was trying to cheer her up a bit, you know, like you do.

'No!' she yelled. Then she said, in a quieter voice, as if she was sorry for shouting, 'I couldn't look at a friggin' cup of tea, Sammie,' but still she wasn't talking to me, she was talking into the sleeping bag, I could hardly hear her, so I couldn't.

'Caroline,' says I, because I was starting to get a bit

worried about her, you know, 'if you can't look at even a cup of tea, there must be something wrong. What is it?'

No answer. Not a word out of her.

'Look, I'll tell you what,' I said then. 'I'll make it fresh and very hot and I'll give you the first cup out, very light and weak, just pale brown water, okay? I won't put milk in it even, it'll be just like flavoured water, okay? That can't disagree with you, whatever is wrong with you. okay, Caro?'

A sound came from the sleeping bag. She might have been agreeing with me, or then again she might have been groaning, but I took it as a yes anyway, so I did.

I wonder what's wrong with her. She must have done something. I bet it was something Beano gave her. He's always getting her to try stuff, so he is. He's trying to turn her into a junkie, that's the long and the short of it. I swear to God, he wants to bring everyone down to his level.

Anyway, before I went off to make the tea, I changed out of the skirt and tights, so I did. I folded the skirt up nice and neat, because I didn't want to crease it, I didn't really feel it was mine, so I laid it on the back of a chair and I rolled the tights loosely and I tucked them under the waistband of the skirt.

Funny that, her giving me the skirt, just chucking it at me. It can't be just because she's not feeling too good. That's a stupid reason to give away your best clothes, so it is. Maybe she had a fight with Beano. That must be it, I think. And she doesn't want the skirt, because he gave it to her, so fair play to her, she sees it like a sort of a love-token, and now she doesn't want it. That could explain why he was so nasty about it too. He must have realised that her giving it to me meant she was rejecting him. I swear to God, I should have been one of them psycho-whatever-you-call-it, psychiatric, is that it? (No, that's a sort of hospital.) Whatever you call it, I'm great at analysing people, so I am. Maybe I'd get a job as an agony aunt in a magazine, giving people advice that write in. That'd be a great job, so it would, but I suppose you'd need a typewriter, or a computer even. I don't think they'd let you just write it all out in a copy with a biro, would they? Probably not.

[CUT TO –]

Red-haired young man with a shaved head, partly grown out, eye-brow ring, sleeveless jerkin and combat trousers, HEAD TO CAMERA.

Curly

I dunno really. Sometimes it's hard to know, isn't it? Why things happen, or how, or whose fault it is, or whatever. I find it hard to know, anyway. It's always somebody's fault, though, I find that's the way people think anyway, somebody always has to take the blame, right. I dunno why they think that. Sometimes I think maybe things just happen and it's no one's fault, right, but other people don't agree with me about that. I dunno, they must be right, I think, though I don't understand it, because other people usually *are* right, that's what I find, anyway. It's hardly ever me that's right, that's what I find. I dunno why. It's hard to know, isn't it?

There's a lot of stuff I don't understand, right, but the main thing is I understand that I don't understand, and that's good if you're like me, right, and you find things hard to work out. That's what Samantha says anyway. She says, 'The great thing about you, Curly, is that you understand that you don't understand, and that's a start anyway.' I don't understand that either, to be honest, but Samantha understands lots of things. She's great, Samantha is.

She says it comes from growing up rough, right. I don't know how rough she grew up, because she won't talk about it, or not much. I mean, look what happened the night she turned up here with young Johnner. She just breezes in, right, and announces this young fella's staying the night, that he had nowhere. Some long night that turned out to be. He's terrible small, you know, and thin, Johnner is, like somebody put a skin-suit one size too small on a skeleton and called it a boy. He's like them skeleton string-puppets they sell in the joke shop, right, always dancing and bobbing and jerking around, you don't even need to pull the strings, you just touch one bit of the skeleton, right, and the whole thing starts into this massive ducking and bobbing and swaying, never stops, one bit of the skeleton hits off another bit of the skeleton and it's into a sort of perpetual motion thing, right, all the bits of the skeleton bashing away against each other and every bit starting every other bit off again, till you get dizzy looking at the thing, and you wish somebody would just grab it with both hands and stop it, see.

Sometimes I want to do that to what's-his-face, Johnner, grab him and press his arms against his sides, see, just for five minutes, so he stops jigging around and making me seasick just from looking at him. He's terrible annoying, that way, the way he keeps bobbing around, but then he sort of gets to you, you know, I dunno why, because he's so full of shit, I think. That's mad, isn't it, that you could nearly like someone because they're full of shit. What I mean is, he gets so carried away, right, with his mad ideas and so excited and everything, that you want to smile. Soft I am, I know, but there it is. That's me. It's hard to know, isn't it?

But he really is full of shit, a stream of *total* garbage comes out of him. The trick is not to try to follow it, right, or you're sunk. Once you realise it's garbage, you're much better off, stands to reason, then it's only like the noise an insect makes, buzz-buzz, all around the room. If you make the mistake of thinking he might be making any kind of sense, then you end up with a fierce headache from trying to listen, see, and put it all together into some sort of normal talk. That's what does your head in, right, trying to make sense of it.

I *knew*, though, I *told* Samantha he was going to be a problem, that we'd be stuck with him, see, once we took him in. It's not that I've anything against the young fella personally, like I say, I kind of like him really, but I said to Sam that if she brought home every waif and stray she found on the streets, right, the place would be like a feckin' orphanage in no time, stands to reason. (I didn't say feckin' either, but I was brung up better than to use bad language, unless I'm upset, of course, which is different.) And then, oh sweet Jesus, she blew her top. She said, 'So what's wrong with an orphanage? Have you got something against people that came out of orphanages or wha'?' Fit to be tied, she was.

Her eyes was all scrunched up when she said that, as if the sun was shining in them or something, see, and her hair was standing out like an electrified mop, like the bride of Frankenstein, she looked, and her fingers too, her hands all stiff and her fingers standing out, right, in as wide a span as she could make, like a cartoon person that got an electric shock. I thought I would have to touch her, put my finger on that little knobbly bone at her wrist, to sort of earth her, like, but then I thought I might get electrocuted too, and anyway, she looked kind of brittle, as if the slightest touch would make bits of her body break off, see? It's hard to know what to do when she gets like that.

Anyway, it's not the kids coming out of them places I'd worry about, I dunno, it's the ones that are running them, the nuns, or brothers, or social workers, or whatever, they're usually nutters. It's logical, isn't it? Only a nutter would want to spend their life looking after other people's kids, day and night, stands to reason. Looking after your own kids is hard enough – I know, because I seen it, women stuck with their kids all day and they end up like two-year-olds themselves – which is why I reckon it's the ones in charge in them orphanages are the ones to worry about, right. Bonkers they are, the whole lot of them, stands to reason. The only thing I've got against anyone out of an orphanage is that it's them nutcases that brung them up, right, instead of the common or ordinary working-class nutcases that brung up the rest of us.

So anyway, I steer well clear of sensitive subjects like orphanages and families and where people come from and all that stuff now when I'm talking to Samantha. I dunno, but it is just something you don't talk to her about. I mean, you could start a forest fire just by *saying* something, using a word people don't like. I mean, I don't mind a good row, but I'd rather it was about something sensible, see? Actually, I don't much like rows anyway, right, and I hate seeing Samantha all upset like that. I don't like to see anyone upset, really, which is why I didn't really object to young Johnny, see, even though I knew we'd end up looking after him, I just knew it, because he has nobody, right, only us now, and he should really be at school, he's only a kid. I mean, none of us is exactly on the old-age pension here, but that young fella is hardly out of national school. It's all wrong. He has a ma and da and all, but he won't go home. He won't tell us why. I suppose the da beats up on him or something, I dunno.

So we're stuck with him now, as if things weren't complicated enough, but sure I suppose that's the way it is. You have to look out for people, don't you, or there's no point at all, is there? So we do, we look out for each other. Most of us do, anyway.

Apart from Beano, of course.

The big difference between me and Samantha is not that she understands things and I don't – that's only a small difference, really, because I understand enough, when it comes down to it – the big difference is that Samantha grew up rough and there is still a bit of her that is all roughed up inside herself because of that, but I grew up rough in a different sort of way, I mean not in an orphanage or nothing, I suppose that's different, really, but anyway, I don't think it left that same kind of mark on me, if you know what I mean. That's how I see it, anyway.

Take my ma, now, for example. I mean, she's not your dream mother, but I don't blame her for that, see what I mean? She was very young when she had me, right, far too young, and she never really got to grips with it, see, being a mother and all, I mean. At the same time, she *was* a mother, whether she liked it or not, and that meant she didn't get to be a girl when she was *supposed* to be a girl. So she couldn't be a girl because she was a mother, see, and she couldn't be a proper mother either, because she was only a girl, that's the way I look at it. Sure how could she?

And then there was me, and I dunno, I think I was always a bit of a problem, so she told me anyway. I was slow to walk, slow to talk, see, always behind the other children, embarrassing her, slow at school, not slow enough to be in the special class, but not fast enough really for the ordinary class either, see, always behind, always struggling. I didn't mind. I dunno, I would be quite happy taking forever to work out my sums, because the thing was – and other people didn't seem to *get* this, for some reason – I *did* work them out in the end, see? That's the way I look at it, anyway.

The way I look at it is this. There's some people that's plain stupid, right, and God love them they will never be able to work anything out no matter how often you tell them, see, and them's the ones that people call 'slow' and they get put in the slow learners class, see? And then there's people like me. I'm not stupid, right, not really dead stupid, but I *am* slow. Dead slow. Slow to get the hang of things. But I *do* get the hang of them in the end, see, if I get enough time. That's the difference, the way I look at it anyway, between slow and stupid.

The problem is, though, that you are not supposed to *call* anyone stupid, I dunno, I suppose it's because it hurts their feelings or something, and I understand that, really I do, of course it is awful to be called stupid, horrible it is, I know what it feels like. But what happens then is that all the *really* stupid ones get called slow, instead of stupid, and then the ones like me, that really *is* slow, but not stupid, they get called slow too, which is fair enough because we *are* slow, but then you see people *think* that because you're *called* slow, that means you're stupid, right? But it doesn't mean that, not really, because it's not the same thing. See? That's the way I look at it, anyway.

That's really very complicated, but I've thought about it for a long time, and I think I'm right about it. It was when I had it all worked out, the difference between slow and stupid, that I knew for sure I was only slow and not stupid, because I thought to myself if I could work all that out for myself, then I couldn't be stupid, could I? Because it is such a complicated thing to work out, see? That's the way I look at it, anyway. It's hard to know, but I think I'm right.

It's so complicated that most people don't even know about it, only the slow people like me, see?

What I think is this: that the quick ones *miss* some of the complicated ideas – I dunno, I think maybe it's because they are so quick, flying around from one thing to the next, getting things done, thinking quick thoughts, jumping to conclusions, right, finding answers before they even know they've got a problem, but, see, they're so busy thinking fast, that they miss some of the *real* complicated ideas, because the complicated ideas are ones you have to think *slowly* about. That is what complicated *means*. That's the way I look at it, anyway.

It's like undoing a knot, see? You can't undo a knot by flying at it and pulling hard. That only makes it worse, see. To untie a knot you have to move slowly, *real* patient like, and tug at the strings *gently*, so you don't make things worse, see? Complicated ideas are the same as knots. If you worry away at them quietly for a while, you start to get the hang of them. There's lots of stuff I don't understand, right, but I think it's only because I haven't had time to think about it yet, because I think slowly.

Samantha, now, is one of the quick ones, and that's good for me, see, because she thinks fast enough for the two of us. I didn't explain to her about the difference between slow and stupid, because I think if I started to tell her it might come out all wrong, it might even sound as if I was sort of *boasting*, and that would be awful, so I keep it to myself. But I do think about it a lot.

I was saying about my ma, and how she had me and it made her life so hard for her, when she was so young and all. Sometimes I think maybe it was the same for Samantha's ma, only she wasn't *that* young, but she found it hard too, being a mother when she didn't really want to be. Mind you, Samantha's ma and da were married. She's very quick to point that out. Makes a fuss about that. I don't really see why that makes any difference. She ended up in care anyway, so what odds does it make, but it's a matter of pride with her.

Although sometimes I do think her parents being married makes it harder for her to understand why she had to go into care, and that's why she goes on about it so much. I think she, well, sort of resents them more as well, because they were married. She thinks they were lucky to have each other and to have her, see, and then they just blew it, over the drink, and that's why she hates them so much, especially her ma. If it was her, she thinks, she would have made a happy home for her husband and her kid instead of drinking herself half to death. She *blames* her ma, see, though it's not really fair, because the da was just as bad, if you listen to what she says about him. But she's one of them people that thinks there's always someone to blame, that things don't just happen, that it's always someone's fault. I think if you think like that, you spend your life blaming people, stands to reason, and you never can just get on with it and forget things, right, and put them behind you. But there you go, we're all different, aren't we? That's the way I look at it anyway.

[CUT TO –]

Young girl, startlingly attractive, wearing a tight T-shirt and short skirt, sitting at a table, with her head resting on her hand, looking glumly out over a mess of unwashed dishes and the remains of a meal.

Caroline

I … I … told Samantha in the end, I had to … I had to tell someone, but I'm not telling Beano … not yet. If I can just hold out … just for a bit … it'll be all right, won't it? I … I … won't tell him till it's too late, and then he'll just have to accept it, won't he? What … what else can he do? Yeah, well … I suppose there's loads of things he can do, aren't there? I … know what he's like … under … all that clever-clever stuff and all that cool-dude stuff, hard as ... hard as, what's dead hard? Diamonds? Yeah, hard as diamonds ... and just as glitzy too. Yeah, I like that. Hard and sparkling, that's Beano ... but no heart, just … just see-through … all the way into … the blinding centre and out the other side ... distorted. Oh God, what am I going to *do*?

But even he … well, I can't think about that now, can I … because if I do, I … won't, I won't be able … to go through with it. I can't even go to the *dentist* for God's sake … or go for a jab or *anything*. I … I … faint in the *waiting* room. I don't even need to *see* a drill or a needle or anything. The *smell* is enough. I just … keel over. Even, even … *thinking* about the smell is nearly enough. And this is, well … it's big-time stuff. I might go into a *coma* and never come out of it. I might … *die*. I … I bet I could die. People used to … all the time. No reason why *I* wouldn't. Oh, what am I going to do?

[PAUSE]

I wish … I wish … I wish my ma was here. I *love* my ma, I do … I did. She was great, my ma. Well, no, to tell the truth, I suppose she wasn't great … not really. She was a *poxy* ma, when I come to think about it. But … she was great all the same. A useless ma … but great *fun*. We used to have such laughs, me and my ma … didn't we? My da used to go … he used to go absolutely *ape*-shit … over the way we would be laughing and giggling over stuff, God I start laughing now even thinking about it. We used to be in the bed, the two of us. I used to get into the bed beside her in the mornings, when he'd be up … getting ready to go to work … and we'd be giggling over *nothing*, wouldn't we … and we'd be laughing so much we'd have to stuff the pillows into our mouths, and he'd get dead mad because we were in bed and he had to go to work, didn't he?

He used … he used … to *roar* at us to shut up and that only made us worse, of course … hearing him roaring … because, because he would threaten awful things, he … he was going to pull us limb from limb … and … and flush us down the *toilet*, and we'd be *screeching* with the laughter, because, you see, because we knew perfectly well he wouldn't as much as ... not as much ... as lay a finger on us, and we'd be *roaring* laughing at the idea of it ... and that would only make him madder, and he'd be so vexed he'd go red with rage, wouldn't he?

'The pipes would get all blocked!' I'd shout, wouldn't I? 'And the Corpo would send somebody around and they'd find detached legs and arms and heads down the toilet! How would you explain that one, heh?' And we'd be off again in more fits of giggles. 'You wouldn't be able to close the toilet seat. There'd be bits of us dribbling blood out onto the bathroom floor!' my ma would add in. 'Hey Da, go on, pull me limb from limb, I dare you!' I'd say. 'Here, start with me foot!'

Oh Jeez, I feel ... Oh Chri ... Oh, I shouldn't be think-ing about blood and guts, it makes my stomach go all ... ooh, there's bile in my mouth and it tastes like cabbage, York cabbage – is that the very green one? or maybe it's kale – oh God, I ... I have to get to the bathroom.

There's no ... Oh Christ, where's the bucket?

It's like doing cold turkey or something. I never ... I never thought it could be this bad. They don't *tell* you it's like this. Your ... your, your skin feels all ... cold and pimply, all the time, and ... your mouth tastes, tastes like you've been eating old pennies. You couldn't, couldn't, couldn't be bothered even, even to comb ... your hair, and you look about a hundred. Also, and this, now this is really ... weird ... your nose feels, feels, feels ... stuffed up all the time, as if you have ... a cold, only you haven't, and your head, your head feels as if it is made of cement, doesn't it?

When I used to be sick when I was small, my … my, my ma used to put her hand on my forehead to see if I, if I … had a temperature. It always made me feel better. I remember too, when I was … really little, I couldn't, couldn't manage my clothes, could I? They were always … always getting in a knot and getting all uncomfortable. My tights used to slip down, didn't they, the way I couldn't walk properly, I was like a … a one-legged person, the middle leg in the three-legged race, and my knickers, they would get into the crack of my bum and my … my vest would be all rucked up, wouldn't it? It used to make me terrible, terrible … terrible crotchety when my clothes got all knotted up, and my ma would say, 'Com'ere to me, you,' and she'd lift my skirt, only she'd do it in a way that it wasn't, wasn't embarrassing, even if, even if there was people around, and she'd pull my knickers straight first and she'd give the waist elastic a little, a little snap against my skin, as if she was telling them … to keep themselves neat, and then she'd pull up my tights properly, so the crotch was *at*, at, at the crotch, not at the knees, and she'd snap the waist elastic on them too, like a little, wasn't it? Then she'd pull my vest down and make sure … it was all under the waist of my skirt … and she'd tuck it into, tuck it into my tights and smooth, smooth it over my stomach and my bum, with a little pat … and then she'd do the same with my jumper, only over my skirt this time, and I would feel like the *neatest* little parcel, wouldn't I, and all the crotchety feelings would go away. That was the best ma-thing she ever done, sett-ling, settling my clothes and putting her hand on my forehead.

Sometimes, Samantha warms up some milk for me … and she puts, she puts a bit of sugar in it, and it's *nearly* like being … small and having your mammy … minding you, only not really. But, but, but I'm glad I told her. It's great that *somebody* knows. God, I'm getting as bad as Johnner, treating Samantha as if she was my ma, amn't I?

Samantha, she has really taken, really, a shine to that young fella. She even, she even tries to make him go to *school* – some hope she has there – and to eat properly. 'You can't be having just chips every day, Johnner,' says she. 'What about an apple?' An apple! I … I ask you, who would give up a bag of chips and have an apple instead? 'I don't have just chips,' Johnner says. 'I often have a burger or a sausage, too.' 'But your *vitamins*, Johnner,' she says. She sounds like, like a teacher or a … social worker or someone. Vitamins!

God, I suppose I should be thinking about my vitamins … now I, I, now I come to think about it, but I … I couldn't as much as … *look* at a bag of chips anyway.

Sometimes, I think he's playing house, Johnner, I mean, Johnner. It's all just, just, just a big game to him, and … he has two sets of mammies and daddies … and he's the little fella … and he's just fooling around like a young one with a, with a teaset, going on about the *curtains* and the tea chest table we have and the slates off the roof and everything, like … like … well, like an adult I suppose. I mean, he's like a small child, a small child playing at being a grown-up and having his own house.

But it's not a game living like this and it's no joke either. It's horrible sometimes, really horrible …

[PAUSE]

I saw a *rat* in the kitchen last week. A rat, and it was as big, as big, as big … as a Jack Russell. I nearly died, didn't I? I screamed … and I threw, I threw, I just threw my shoe at it, but it … didn't move. It just sat there, *looking* at me, with its horrible little whiskers, just sort of *quivering* and, and, and its little red eyes piercing me, it felt like. When I threw the shoe, it blinked, and it went on quivering.

I thought I was – I really thought I was going to throw up, I felt that sick looking at it, but then I had this really gross idea that if I did, the rat would just, just sit there and calmly *eat* it, in front of me, and I knew that if it did that I would … I definitely would just die, just die on the spot, and that, I swear, is the only thing, the only thing that kept me from throwing up. So then I … I screamed again, didn't I, and this time it sort of, sort of waddled off, slowish, into a corner of the room, and then it sat there again, and it was still quivering in that awful way, so you knew it was alive, didn't you?

Beano, he came in then, I think he must've heard the screams. 'What's up, love?' he says, in that con*cern*ed voice he puts on sometimes, sometimes, when he's playing Mr Nice Guy. I couldn't speak, could I? I couldn't even *point* at the rat. I … I tried to raise my hand, but it wouldn't move for me. It was like that feeling you get sometimes when, sometimes when you have a nightmare and you, you can't move.

But Beano, he could see that I was staring at

something, something in the corner, so he hunkers down, just hunkers down ... and has a squint. It was nearly, nearly dark in the kitchen. Not pitch black like night-time, it was only about dinnertime, but it was one of them very grey days, very grey, with rain and clouds and hardly any light out, only a sort of a gleam in the sky, that ... that, that mustardy-coloured light you get sometimes, so like I said, the corner, the corner of the kitchen was all shadowy, you could hardly see, hardly see, except you *could* see the quivering in the little bit of light there was.

It took Beano, it took him a minute or two to see the rat, I think, but when he did ... he stood up, stood up real slow ... and he held his hands out in front of him, out in front of him, and he sort of dusted his palms off each other a few times, you know, like a gangster in a film, in that 'I-mean-business' sort of way.

I was staring at the rat, just staring at it, I couldn't stop looking at it, like it had some sort of *power* over me, but again I heard that whispery sound of Beano, of him wiping his hands off each other ... I turned to look at him, and I swear it looked as if ... as if *he* was quivering too, just like the rat. God, it was spooky, it was nearly totally silent in the room but then I could hear a bubbly sound and a sort of, a sort of a hiss in the background, and for a second I thought it was the *rat* hissing, but then I remembered ... well, I remembered that I'd come into the kitchen to boil a pot of water. It must be boiled, I thought to myself, it must be boiled.

The next thing, Beano, he reached over and picked up

the pan of boiling water, oh Christ ... and he aimed it right at the rat. I mean, he didn't stop, he didn't hesitate for a second, he just did it all nearly in one movement, didn't he? I closed my eyes as hard as I could, I didn't want to see the rat going for him, it was horrible, so I just concentrated on trying to count the little purply blobs I could see behind my eyelids, but I could still hear, I couldn't shut my ears, could I? First I could hear the slosh, the slosh of the water as it rose out of the pot, the way it bucketed down and then there was, there was the most godawful squeal, and this terrible, this really terrible scrabbling sound of the rat ... running on the lino. It's going for the jugular now, for sure, I was thinking ... the jugular ... that's what they say about rats, don't they, that they know where to aim for, they kill people that way.

Oh God, horrible it was, horrible ... the sound of its claws scratching on the lino, and I still had my eyes closed, and I was thinking, thinking here it comes now, it's going to ... it's going to attack. But then the sound of the claws got slower and slower and sort of faded away, and again I opened my eyes, the rat ... the rat was lying on the floor, there it was, it was only about a foot away, only about a foot, from where it had been when Beano threw the boiling water at it, and it was sort of pawing the ground and *twitching*, but I could see that it was dead, or as near to dead as made no difference.

There was all water, all water ... everywhere ... running into the corners of the room and dripping down between the floor and the skirting board. I knew that because, because, because I could hear this dripping sound. And it was steaming ... the water ... because it was just off the boil, like. Even the rat was steaming, and there was a horrible musty smell, like that raincoaty smell you get on a bus on a wet day, desperate it smelt.

'God, Beano, you killed it!' I sort of croaked. I was still staring at it, at the rat. I couldn't take my eyes off it.

'Yeah,' said Beano, and then I turned to look at him, and he had this big, this great big satisfied grin across his face, hadn't he?

The next thing I knew I was on the floor. I don't think I really fainted ... not really, but my knees just sort of gave way ... just gave way under me, and down I went, right into the pool of hot water. It had spread out a good distance by now, hadn't it? Lucky it had cooled down a bit, or I'd have been scalded, wouldn't I? I wasn't scalded, but I was soaked, I can tell you.

'Here, Caro, get up can't you,' said Beano, but he said, he said it in a sort of a *tender* voice, you know that way, when someone is being nice, being nice, and it sounded real, as if he really was being nice, and he put out his hand to me. I grabbed onto his hand and he heaved me up.

'Sorry,' I said. 'I don't know what happened, my, my knees ...'

'All right, all right, but did you hurt yourself?' he asked, looking into my face.

'No, I'm fine,' I said, though I could feel that I'd given my hip a right crack where I fell sort of half onto my side. My shoulder, it felt sore too, I think I must've been puttin' out a hand to save myself and given it a wrench.

'Here,' said Beano, 'I'll take you into the bedroom so you can change. Have you dry clothes to put on?'

He put his hand under my elbow and he put his other arm around, around my waist, and just before we moved off he put his cheek on my hair, on my hair, oh, lovely it was, kind of all wistful you know, and I closed my eyes and I felt these lovely sensations running through me.

Since I've been feeling sick, I haven't felt a bit like that. If somebody, a fella I mean, touches me now, it just makes me feel, just makes me feel all shivery and goose-pimply instead of making me feel all warm and wibbly. But just then, for once, I got that lovely feeling like one of them really amazing fireworks, like it's going off inside you in slow motion – don't laugh, that's what it feels like – first you get this hot rush and then, and then, the feelings all spread out, all sort of warm and prickly and sort of *sparkly*. Feeling like that, feeling like that is what got me mixed up with Beano in the first place, I know, and now look at me.

But anyway, I moved my head under Beano's cheek … and I snuggled in to his neck, and then I put a little tiny kiss, just a tiny little kiss, on his throat and he squeezed with his hand, where it lay just above my other hip … and then, then he gave me a little stroke, as if I was a kitten or something small and precious. It was nice to feel precious … precious, for a change. Most of the time, most of the time … I feel cheap, when I think of how low I've sunk sometimes, how low.

I was nearly going to tell him then, when we were

standing there, all kind of close and friendly, but ... but something stopped me, I don't know what. Instead, I made a stupid joke: 'My hero,' I whispered, I mean, I was sending him up really, sending him up ... though I have to admit, I nearly half meant it at the same time.

He looked down at me and he has this stupid big grin on his face, this big stupid grin, dead pleased with himself he was, I don't think he realised I was poking fun at him ... though as I say ... if I'm honest, if I'm honest, I was half serious about it, wasn't I?

'Come on, Caroline, you'll catch your death in them wet clothes,' says he, and he's walking me, walking me out of the kitchen and towards the bedroom. 'Get yourself into something dry now, okay.'

I ... I ... I could hardly believe he didn't try to take advantage. Then I began to wonder was there something *wrong* that he didn't. That was a bit confusing, a bit confusing ... but still I was more glad than confused, because I was feeling sick again and cold from the wet clothes, cold and shivery, far colder than just a wetting should've made me, and I certainly didn't want any of *that*, sparkly feelings or no sparkly feelings. I know where that gets you, that's for sure, don't I just?

He probably thought I was feeling wobbly because of the rat, the rat, you know, and that's why he let me be, and to tell the truth the rat did make me feel sicker, especially that dreadful squeal and then the panicky scrabbling, scrabbling of the claws on the lino. It makes me ... go ... all shuddery, all shuddery when I think about it, even now. Eughh!

That was a few days ago, and every night since I've dreamt about rats, hundreds of them, like in the story about the piper fella, rats running all over the place, like a plague. I wake up in the middle of the night, imagining them scuttling over me, scuttling over me in the dark, one or two of them wriggling down into the sleeping bag beside me. Sometimes, sometimes I dream about rats and babies all mixed up together, a rat attacking a baby in a pram, eating its poor little face off, and the baby is crying and crying but nobody can hear it ... and then I scream and I wake myself up ... and my heart, my heart is thundering away like a train and every nerve in my body, that's what it feels like, every nerve ... is screaming at me and I, then I have to make myself breathe real slow ... real slow, and deep, deep, and I keep telling myself it's just a dream, but I know that it's not just a dream, that these things can happen, that there really was a rat and that if Beano hadn't got it first, it might have got us. Ugh!

[PAUSE]

You know, after that rat episode, I was nearly beginning to feel different about Beano, but then that bloody party happened and everything changed, or maybe it didn't really. Maybe ... maybe it was just the same, only it was clearer then, the way things are, the way they are.

God, it was awful. Worse than if it was my *parents*, for God's sake, my parents. But I mustn't think about them, or I will only start crying. Imagine them if they knew! I wonder what ... no, I mustn't, I won't.

Johnner had been drivelling on and on about it and driving us all doolally, absolutely doolally. He's like that, he drones on about things, drones on about them ... and keeps yacking away, like an insect buzzing around the room and driving you crazy, so in the end you'd say yes to anything, yes to anything, just to shut him up, and that's how it happened, I suppose, he just wore us all down and we said yes, Johnner, we'll have a bleedin' party if it makes you happy, okay? So that's how it happened, really, that we went ahead and had the party. It was kind of nice, at first, sort of relaxing, you know ...

[MUSIC and FADE OUT]

PART 2

johnner's party

FADE IN

INTERIOR: THE SQUAT 'BEDROOM' – EVENING

It's dark but lit by candles. PAN around the room.
Empty. But gradually the room begins to fill with
sounds, scuffling sounds, a door slamming,
laughter, whoops, people having a good time,
someone inexpertly plucking a guitar.

CUT TO Samantha, speaking TO CAMERA.

Samantha

Curly invited two fellas off this Youthreach course he's
doing to Johnner's party, so he did. Johnner invited his
sister Lorraine. Nobody else invited anyone. Well, I
haven't got any friends, except Curly. I had a friend
called Sally, but she went to Birmingham, so she did, to
her auntie over there. And Caro was afraid of what
Beano would say if *she* invited someone, and Beano
didn't invite anyone because he wasn't coming himself,
or so he said. He said he had *business* to attend to that

night. He's always talking about business, so he is. You'd swear he was a tycoon the way he does be going on.

I wore the skirt Caroline gave me, and this little strappy top I have, it's sort of silvery and shimmery, and of course I had the tights Caro gave me and this pair of platform sandals I got off that girl I used to know, Sally. She said they were too small for her. They let in the rain, but it doesn't matter inside. In fairness, now, I have to say I looked very nice, so I did.

Caroline wore a dress, a sort of shift. It's dark red, but it has a raised pattern on it, in black, so it has. It's nice, with a little V-neck. She says it's more comfortable than a skirt now. She looked good in it, though then again her face is very drawn looking, with all the getting sick. She didn't drink and she didn't smoke.

One of Curly's mates, Gerry his name is, he brought a bottle of Smirnoff to the party, fair play to him, wherever he got it. I made Caro some tea, very hot and weak, and she poured the tiniest drip of the vodka into it, and she sipped at that. She said it tasted funny, so she did, but it didn't make her sick. Tea with vodka would make me sick, I think, and I'm perfectly well, but there you go.

One of Curly's mates off the course brought his guitar, not the one that brought the vodka, the other one. He can only play three chords, he said, because he's only learning, but I couldn't tell the difference, anyway. I'm not musical, me, I like all the wrong bands, I even like the Spice Girls. It sounded very nice to me the way he strummed away at it, it did. Come to think of it, I suppose it didn't sound like actual music, but it was the kind of noise you don't mind listening to, you know? He sang a bit too, but his voice is croaky, nearly like as if it hasn't changed properly yet, though it sounded okay when he was talking, so it did, and he's nearly eighteen. Maybe it's got something to do with the style of singing, maybe it's *meant* to sound like that, to make it more … 'meaningful', I suppose. It wasn't what you would call *cheerful* music, but still it was nice, so it was.

There used to be someone I knew when I was younger, somebody in the home where I used to live, one of the people that looked after us, Brian was his name, he had a ponytail and he used to play the guitar for us sometimes, so he did, and sing, and he'd get us all singing the chorus. It reminded me of that. Those were good times, them evenings when we'd sit around the fire and sing songs and Brian used to make us all do a party-piece, but I couldn't sing so I'd tell a ghost story, so I would.

We had a fire for the party too, I mean, for Johnner's party. There's a fireplace in the bedroom, but we never lit a fire in it before, because we thought the chimney would probably be blocked, and we don't really want the whole street to find out we're here by having a chimney fire. I mean, nobody much lives around here, and the ones that do probably know we're here anyway, but even so, a chimney fire would not be what you would call very diplomatic.

The day before the party, Johnner had a dry run. He burned a whole lot of papers in it, so he did, and they burnt fine. It smoked a bit, but not too badly, so then we went looking for stuff to put on the fire. We hunted in skips, so we did, and we brought home old broken-down chairs and bits of packing cases and rotten floorboards and all sorts of things, and we got a real blaze going, it was great. Johnner got carried away and he wanted to chop up the tea chest too, so he did, but I stopped him. 'We need that for a table, Johnner,' says I. I swear to God, if I left him at it, that young fella'd have the whole place burnt down around us, so he would.

It was great to have a fire. I nearly toasted myself, so I did. I spent the whole evening sitting in front of it, so I did, and feeding bits of wood into it. I was supposed to be minding it and making sure the sparks didn't jump out and set the house on fire, because some of the wood was damp and it made a lot of crackles and sent out showers of sparks, but really I was enjoying getting every square inch of me warm for the first time in months. My hair still smells of woodsmoke after it, so it does, but it was worth it, really it was.

The fire made the room all rosy and cosy. (There, I'm a poet and I knew it all along.) It was like a room in a story, so it was, all shadows, and there was these fiery reflections lepping over the walls, so there were. And then Johnner, fair play to him, he lit up his candles. He must have had dozens of them, I swear to God, they were dotted all over the place, and they twinkled all over the room, it was like Christmas, so it was. Darren, he was crooning away, and people were drinking and laughing and smoking and their cigarettes made little red glowing spots, dots really, in the room. They looked like tiny back bicycle lights, wobbling in the dark.

I told one of my ghost stories from when I was small, and everyone huddled together and screamed when I got to the scary bits and giggled, and Brian, no, I mean Darren, he made spooky sounds on his guitar, you know, playing one note after the other – what do you call that, when the notes are nearly the same as each other, but still a little bit different, and they are going up and up and up like climbing the stairs? – only of course Darren could only make a few notes, so he could, and he had to repeat the same ones a few times, but we didn't mind. We sat around on the sleeping bags and we went 'Wooooh!' and we drank neat vodka.

I *never* drink vodka because once I did when I was fourteen and I was sick for a week after it, so I was, and I swore I was going to become a Pioneer, but of course I didn't. Still, I never drank vodka since, until last night. It tasted horrible, because he hadn't any mixers to put in it, and it really wasn't a good idea, drinking it neat, I mean. Now I remember why I swore I'd never drink it again. Still, it was a great night, so it was, and that's a fact, and even Johnner's oul' fags weren't as stale as they looked, or anyway they didn't taste stale after the vodka.

After a while, we'd burnt all the wood we'd gathered, and I thought we were going to get cold – you know me and the cold – but I suppose the body heat in the room had built up by then, so even with just the embers we were still grand and warm, so we were. Then Johnner, he lit a fresh batch of candles, and the room was all flickering again with little golden lights, and it smelt lovely and, what's the word? – fragrant, that's it, fragrant – from the candles and the smouldering wood, nearly like incense, lovely it was.

By this stage I'd had a few vodkas, you know, and the room was starting to move a bit, the way it does, and the candles were running into each other and shifting around. That was when I should've stopped drinking, so I should, if I didn't want to get the horrors, but sure I was enjoying myself that much that I just filled up a cup and I went on sloshing it back, so I did. Very stupid.

Next thing, I have to admit, I was nodding off. Curly was lying out flat on his back in front of the fireplace, fair play to him, with a bottle of the red wine beside him, and every now and then he'd sit up and take a slug out of it, and then lie down again. I started to get very sleepy, and I settled my head on his chest. I could hear his heart beating under my ear, so I could. It was like a horseman coming from a long way away. 'You have a horse in your chest, Curly, a horse and jockey,' I murmured to him and he giggled. 'Yeah, I have a whole racecourse in there,' says he, and he opened his arms and pulled me right down beside him. That was the last thing I remember, because then I dozed off for a while.

When I woke up, I swear to God, I didn't know *where* I was. The fire was dead. The room had got cold and dark. But then again it seemed to be full of people, far more than before I fell asleep, but I couldn't see them, so I couldn't, because of the dark and because I'd just woken up. Somebody was screaming, a woman, I didn't know whether it was Lorraine or Caroline, and then the screams turned into sobs and screams mixed together.

There was all these noises, like lurching and shouting going on, and I could hear Beano's voice, so I could. 'Bitch!' he was shouting. It was coming from the next room. 'Bitch, slut, slapper.' Then I knew it was Caroline who was screaming and I scrambled to my feet, and I kicked at Curly to wake him up, so I did.

'Curly,' says I with a hiss, like this, 'wake up, wake up, Beano's beating up Caroline and she'll lose the baby if he hits her in the stomach.'

But suddenly I sat down again with a thud so I did. The room was starting to *reel* around me, even though I couldn't see it. I felt as if I was on a chair-o-plane ride at a carnival. I should've stuck to the beer. I know where I am with beer, so I do.

Curly sat up. I could see now in the dark, because my eyes had got used to it, and one of Johnner's candles was still spitting away on the mantelpiece. Curly's face was all creased down one side, and there was a pattern on the skin, you know like frost makes on the window in cold weather, where he'd fallen asleep with his cheek against my hair.

'Baby?' says he, as if I'd said 'bomb'. He was running his fingers through his hair, making it all stick up even more than usual. 'What baby? Whose baby?' Of course, he didn't know about the baby.

'God, will you shut it, Curly,' says I. 'Don't ask, just don't ask. Get up and get Beano *off* her.' It really wasn't the time or the place for a conversation like that so it wasn't, I mean, I *ask* you.

Caroline had stopped screaming now and she'd stopped sobbing too, so she had. I remember thinking, I hope she's not dead, because there was this awful silence after she stopped screeching, so there was, except it wasn't really silent, because every now and then I could hear Beano thumping her, thump, thump, thump, it had a rhythm to it, like a soldier doing a work-out or something.

Anyway, so Curly stumbles to his feet, and he swayed for a bit. He must have had a lot of that red wine, because he doesn't usually sway after a few scoops, so he doesn't, but at least it wasn't as bad as the vodka, I reckon, because there was no way I could've stood up, not if you paid me, not if Caroline started to go into *labour* right there and then.

It was when I thought that word, 'labour', that it really hit me how serious this was. Where was Johnner, I wondered. And Darren and what was the other bloke's name? When I woke up, I thought the room was full of people, but maybe it was just the sounds from the next room that gave me that impression. So anyway, I started squeezing up my eyes, so I did, and really peering into the shadows, like this, to see if there was anyone else in the room, but then the last candle on the mantelpiece makes this little spluttery noise, and out it goes, great, just what we needed.

Next thing I hear Johnner's voice in my ear, 'Saman-tha, Samantha, Samantha!' He was shouting, only in a whisper, if you see what I mean, it's kind of hard to explain. 'Oh Jesus, Samantha, he's after *killing* her.' He was crying, so he was, I could hear it in his voice, though I couldn't really see his face.

'Johnner,' says I. 'Shsh, shsh, shush crying now, because I want you to do something for me,' says I. I was thinking very clearly, fair play to me, considering I couldn't even stand up. 'Were you drinking, Johnner?'

'I only had a can of cider, I swear,' Johnner said, as if I was his *ma*, for God's sake, giving him the third degree after coming in late.

'Good, so you're sober, more or less,' says I. 'Now listen, Curly's gone to try and stop Beano, but Curly is maggoty, so he is. And Beano is probably *flying* on something, whatever that stuff is that he does.'

Then we heard a dreadful crash. Well, it was more like a thud than a crash, but it was an almighty sound anyway, Jaysus, you'd think the *roof* was after coming in, and it could easily, it's a poxy old roof, so it is. Next thing, Johnner runs into the next room, which is the kitchen, and I started to crawl after him.

It was even darker in the kitchen, because it faces out the back, so it does, away from the streetlights, and of *course* we haven't got any electricity, only a flashlamp that we use if we come in at night, but the batteries is flat and nobody has had the money to buy new ones. Well, we wouldn't, would we?

Anyway, there was all this thumping going on and snorting, but I couldn't see who was hitting who, I could only hear. The next thing, I hear Curly's voice coming in gulps: 'Sam – is that – you? Here, help – me with – Beano.' I could hear somebody making sort of angry grunts, only they were all muffled, so they were, and I guessed that must be Beano with his head someplace real uncomfortable, like under Curly's armpit or somewhere, and there's scuffling going on too, like somebody's feet are trying to get a grip on the floor.

I struggled to my feet – in fairness, it really *was* a struggle – and by some miracle I stayed upright, though my head felt as if it was going to lift off my shoulders at any minute, so it did, and go floating up to the ceiling like one of them helium balloons. By now I could make out where the noises were coming from – and it was from this mass of bodies in one corner of the kitchen, really heaving and struggling they were.

Curly had Beano pinned down, so he had, and he was *sitting* on him, but he must've been finding it hard to keep him under control. And from the other side of the room, I could hear Johnner talking real soft and quiet-like to Caroline and Caroline was whimpering out of her, so she was, as if she was a baby or a little puppy or something. Oh God, I remember thinking, I wonder how bad she's hurt? But I couldn't go to her, because Curly needed help to keep Beano under control, so I went and sat on his legs. I realised then that the thumping sounds I could hear were Curly thumping Beano's head off the floor, I swear to God.

'Hey, lay off, Curly,' I roared at him – and all this time, I was riding Beano's kicking legs, I swear I was like a cowboy on a bucking bronco, I can tell you I was feeling dead seasick, so I was. 'You'll kill him if you smash his head like that,' says I.

'I bleedin' well *will* kill him,' says Curly and his voice is real angry like, real angry, not like Curly at all. 'He's a hoorin' bastard.'

'Yes, I know he is,' says I, 'but you don't want to get done for murder, you fat eejit you.'

'I have to knock him out, Sam,' says Curly. 'If I don't we'll have to sit on him all night.'

Knocking him out sounded a bit drastic, so it did, but I could see Curly's point. Anyway, it was too late to argue, because suddenly all the noises stopped, the struggling and kicking stopped, and the scuffling noises just sort of petered out.

'You *are* after knocking him out, Curly,' says I. 'God, I hope he's not *dead*.' I really was scared we'd killed him.

'He's not dead,' said Curly, standing up. 'He's breathing. I can hear him.'

Well, he was *breathing*, only it wasn't natural-sounding; he was taking in these huge gulps of air, so he was, but we couldn't hear him breathing out at all, and then he'd breathe in another big gulp. You'd swear he had a hole in his lungs and he was trying to fill them up, but the air kept on escaping on him. I could just imagine it leaking all over his body, so I could, and making him swell up. It would be awful to die of suffocation with your body full of air, wouldn't it? I nearly began to feel sorry for him, but only nearly.

Great party this turned out to be.

[CUT TO –]

Johnner

I know my party wasn't, like, the main thing, but all the same, I was awful disappointed. I wanted it to be a really, like, magic party, I wanted everyone to have a great time, yeah, for us all to be *happy*, I mean like a *family* together. But it all went wrong on me and I have this awful feeling that it was sort of my fault. I know it wasn't really, but because it happened at my party, I feel sort of responsible. That's stupid, I know, but you can't really control your feelings, can you?

It started off great, we had singing and everything, and I was right about the candles, they were, like, fantastic, just fantastic, it was like a fairy grotto. Once when I was small they took me to see Santy in a fairy grotto, and it was, like, dark, mainly, but there was all these little twinkly lights everywhere and this music – heavenly it was – coming from nowhere. It was like being in another world, where you just sort of floated and looked at the lights and listened to the music and nothing could touch you, nothing could hurt you or harm you.

It was like that, my party, in the beginning, with the candles and the singing and all, and everyone laughing and having a good time. They were passing around something, like, in a cigarette. I didn't have any, because of my chest, which is not great, I have to admit, and anyway it smelt awful (I see why they call it shit), but they were all, like, smiling fit to rip their faces and laughing and making silly little jokes and I was watching them all and feeling real, like, proud because it had all been my idea and I'd got them all there and sort of, you know -

created something, I mean, like a present for my friends, yeah. It was the first time I felt I was able to, like, give them something back. I mean, they've been good to me, they let me live here, even though they're two couples and I'm really just a kid – that's how they see it anyway – and they're great mates, and now it was my turn to do something good for them, yeah. And then bleedin' Beano had to go and, like, spoil everything, with his fighting. He's a bit of a bully is Beano. He *said* he wasn't coming to my stupid kiddies' party. Wanted to know was I going to invite Giggsy and all the lads, ha-ha. I know that sounds a bit hurtful, but that's just the way Beano does be going on, always over-exaggerating everything, has to make anything he doesn't want to be involved in sound really stupid, nothing, just because it's not his idea or his choice or whatever.

So I tried to ignore that. I said, 'That's fine, Beano, cool, as long as you don't mind the rest of us going ahead and having a good time.' He just, like, snorted at that, as if it wasn't possible for anyone to have a good time at something *he* didn't want to be involved in. Sometimes I wonder if that's why he created the way he did, just to spoil it on me. I know that's maybe a funny way of looking at it, but I get this feeling that Beano really doesn't like me much. Anyway, if he did set out to spoil it all, he sure as hell succeeded.

[CUT TO –]

Curly

I dunno, I haven't really figured out yet exactly what happened. It was, well, it was after the party had got to that sort of stage, oh, mellow, I suppose you'd say, the mellow stage, see, when Beano, he comes bollocking into the gaff. Like a demented whirlwind, he was, and then there was just this huge scrap. Caro was crying, right, and Samantha was dead drunk, but she was trying to be sensible, see, only she couldn't make her words come out in the right order, or not in any order *I* could follow, anyway. Lorraine was there and she was feeling a bit the worse for wear too, see.

The next thing, I was beating the shite out of Beano, I mean, really going at him, hammer and tongs like there was no tomorrow, and Samantha was battering away at him as well, screeching out of her like a mad woman.

I thought we'd killed him, I really did, and, you know what it is, at the time I didn't care. I don't usually think of myself as the sort of fella that likes scrapping, right, but, the way I see it is, janey, when I heard Caroline screaming like that, something just flipped in me and I went into, I dunno, another mode or something, and before I knew where I was, I was flailing around with Beano under me.

I wanted to call an ambulance, right, but they wouldn't let me. They said if the ambulance came we'd all be arrested or something, so I said we had to get Beano to casualty, stands to reason, and Samantha shrieked, '*Beano*! Is it Beano you're worried about? It's not Beano that needs a doctor, it's Caroline.' I'd kind of forgotten about Caroline, see, because I was so taken up with thinking we'd murdered Beano between us, but as soon as Samantha mentioned her, I could hear this sort of a whimpering sound in another part of the room – it was dark, the candles was long gone out at this stage, and the torch is broken – and it was Caroline that was making the whimpering noises, see, and she was sort of moaning and talking at the same time. She kept saying over and over, 'My baby, oh, my baby!' I went over to her and I tried to calm her down.

I said, 'Hey, it's okay, Caro, no need to worry about Beano. He's breathing. I think maybe he sort of fainted a bit, but he'll come round now in a minute, wait till you see.' I thought it was sort of sweet that she was so worried about him, but I didn't want her to be upset, right. I don't like it when people are upset.

So I put my hand out to her and oh, sweet suffering saviour, she was all wet and sticky. Blood! Loads of it. Everywhere. God, it was like a butcher's shop.

'Did you fall, Caro?' I asked her, but she just moaned. 'I mean,' this is me now, talking to Caro, 'did you bang your head or something?'

A cut from the head bleeds something terrible, I know that, because it happened to me once, me ma clocked me one – she didn't mean anything, she just lashed out one day when I was annoying her – and I fell against a press door that was open, right, one of them cornery ones with the aluminium edges, you know, and it gashed my head and there was *buckets* of blood, buckets of it there was. They rushed me off to the hospital, see, but it was only a little cut and it didn't even need a stitch, they just put a little clip thing on it, but you'd've thought I was going to bleed to death there was so much blood.

'Oh God, Sam,' I shouted. 'She's covered in blood.'

'Can you look after her, Curly?' says Samantha. 'I have to stay with Beano, make sure he's still breathing, like.'

I kind of dabbed at Caro a bit to see if the blood was coming from her head, but it wasn't. It seemed to be coming from lower down, right, from her belly, I thought. I couldn't imagine how she could scrape her belly that bad, even if there was a press door or something to bang against.

Just then, Beano came round. I could hear him effin' and blindin' to Samantha, and she was talking to him in this low voice, trying to calm him, I suppose, and in between the curses he was groaning about his head hurting and every now and then he gave this shout, right, that sounded like someone roaring in a cave, but he didn't try to stand up or nothing, he'd stopped fighting, he'd just given up.

Then I had a brainwave, right, and I went back into the other room and got the matches. I knew there had to be matches, see, because of the candles, and once I had that thought, I remembered seeing them on the mantelpiece. I had to keep striking them because they went out nearly as soon as they were lit, but there were loads of them so it didn't matter. First, I had a look around the room. Lorraine, that's Johnner's sister, she was at the party too, she was in a corner, and she was moaning a bit. The other pair, Darren and Ger, must've scattered, because there was nobody else in the room. I went over to Lorraine, and as soon as I got close to her, she started saying, real quick, 'I'm all right, I'm fine, I'll stand up in a minute, I'm all right.'

So I went on back into the kitchen, and I struck more matches and after about the fourth one, right, I managed to see that Caro was bleeding from a wound at the front of her shoulder, as if somebody went to stab her in the chest, right, and she sort of dodged down and the knife went in higher up, see.

Knife! Holy God! It was only then it hit me, right, that Beano must've havin' a knife. I lit another match then and I saw it, lying on the floor, and it was one of them Stanley knives, *desperate* things they are, dead sharp, only the blade is short so it can't go right into you. I don't know how he didn't go for me with it, he could've cut my *ear* off or something. Maybe he dropped it when I went for him. Jeez, that was dead lucky. He's a right gurrier is that Beano, that's the way I look at it.

'Oh cripes, Caroline, did he go for you with that yoke?' I asked her, but she just kept mumbling about her baby. I couldn't understand why she was so concerned about him when he was after slicing her up with a Stanley knife.

Next thing, Lorraine appears in the room. I heard her coming, right, and I struck another match and it flared up and there she stood in the doorway, big as a mountain, she looked, and holding onto her belly as if it was going to fall off. She was fairly sober, as far as I could tell.

I don't know why she was moaning before, maybe she was just upset. She told me she tries not to drink too much because of the baby, only the doctor told her that if she smokes and drinks she will have a small baby, and she said, 'That's fine by me, Doc, easier to get it out!' but she was only joking, right. I could tell because she laughed so much when she told me about it. I don't know why that's such a joke. It seems logical to me. Stands to reason.

Lorraine kind of lurched over to me and as soon as she saw the state Caro was in she started swearing out of her worse even than Beano. He'd more or less calmed down by now. She said I was to get her a bandage, right, so anyway I went into the bedroom and I found this packet of Band Aid I have since the time I cut my finger on a broken bottle, see, only she roared at me when I brought it back to her. 'A bandage!' she screeched, 'I need a bleedin' bandage, not a sticking plaster. This is bleedin' *serious*.'

That made me laugh, 'bleedin' serious'. You know how it is, you laugh sometimes when awful things happen, I do anyway, that's me. 'Do you not mean serious bleedin'?' says I to Lorraine, 'instead of bleedin' serious, I mean.' Well, it seemed funny at the time, see. She made a sound like a dog growling when I said that. I never heard a woman making a sound like that before. Brought me back to my senses, it did.

'God, I'm awful sorry, Lorraine,' I said and I beat it into the bedroom, right. So anyway I got a clean white T-shirt and between us – Johnner helped too, even though I could see in the matchlight, right, that he was as white as the T-shirt – anyway, between us we managed to wash the cut with one half of the T-shirt and to bandage it up with the other half, and we got Caro into bed, at least, into her sleeping bag. She seemed to be very drunk, but Lorraine said that was probably concussion, see. I dunno, but maybe that was it.

I know now that you are not supposed to put concussed people to bed, because I read about it in this leaflet called 'Do the Right Thing in an Emergency' – I found it in the Mater casualty – but we didn't know that then. The way I see it, it's a bit stupid to put them leaflets in casualty, because that's where people go *after* they've had an accident, right, when it's too late to Do the Right Thing in an Emergency. It is amazing how stupid people like doctors can be, especially when you think about how clever they are supposed to be – all the exams they have to pass and everything. I dunno.

Anyway, she must be tough, Caroline, because she was fine this morning, see. I mean, she wasn't really fine, the T-shirt bandage was covered in blood, right, and she was screeching every time she moved with the pain of the cut, but her head was okay, she didn't die of concussion in the night or she didn't have a brain haemorrhage or whatever it is that you get if you go to sleep after a bang on the head because your mates don't know how to Do the Right Thing in an Emergency. She was still going on about her baby, and I told her Beano was okay, just to calm her down, though I knew he wasn't there, he'd legged it in the night, I think, when we were all trying to fix Caroline up, anyway he wasn't here this morning, see.

And then Samantha woke up, right, and she got into my sleeping bag with me, because she was so cold, and she whispered to me that Caro was pregnant. I couldn't believe it.

'She *can't* be,' I said, 'she's too *thin*.' I was thinking of Lorraine, carrying her bump in front of her like the cab of an articulated truck.

'You eejit you,' says Samantha, in that loving way she has, I don't think. 'You don't get fat straight away, dickhead. It takes time to grow a bump. And anyway, she *is* fatter. That's why she gave me her good skirt.'

It took me a while to work that one out. She's not fat but she is fat, is what Samantha seemed to be saying. I mean, what do I know about it? I've never been pregnant. I haven't got any sisters, right. I've only had a girlfriend for a month. I just never thought about it. And then I had a horrible moment of panic: 'You're okay, Sam, aren't you?' I asked her.

'Of course I am, you stupid sap you.'

I didn't think that was a very sappy question, really, but she just calls me things like out of habit, see. She doesn't necessarily mean them. But anyway, then I began to understand why Caro kept going on about her baby, and why Samantha nearly died when I told her Caroline was all blood last night. It was dark, right, and we couldn't see where it was coming from. Sam must've thought Caro was losing the baby. I think Caro must've thought that too, because of the way she kept going on about it, but she was concussed, so she probably didn't know what it was all about. I dunno.

She's okay this morning, but me and Sam, right, we took her over to the Mater anyway, as soon as she was fit to walk, because Samantha thought the cut might go septic, see. They put some stinging stuff on it and some cream and a proper bandage. Of course they wanted to know what had happened and all the rest of it, we had a terrible time getting them just to fix her up without having to tell them our life story.

Caroline was terrified of going near a hospital in case they found out that she's pregnant and living rough, right, but I told her they wouldn't notice she's pregnant, no way – I never noticed, I said, and she gave this sarcastic laugh, see. I dunno why she laughed like that, but anyway, I said we'd make up an address. 'We'll use Lorraine's address,' I said. 'Lorraine said we could.' She didn't, but I had to say that to get Caroline to agree to go, see. In the end she said she would, but only because she needed painkillers, see.

So we gave Lorraine's address anyway, and they wrote it down, but they still kept going on with questions about what happened and how did she get cut and who did it and did we report it to the guards and all this stuff. They're always like that, these people. They can never just do their bandages and needles and medicine and stuff, right. They always want to take you over like invading aliens or something. Why can't they just let us get on with it? I mean, the way I see it, if you go to have your shoes fixed, the bleedin' cobbler doesn't want to know how you got them so scuffed, does he? No, he bleedin' doesn't. If you call in the plumber, he doesn't want to know why your pipes are rusty, does he, he just fixes them, right? So why do these doctory people want to know your every move? Why can't they just do what they know about and sew you up? I don't know. I don't understand it at all.

But anyway, they fixed her up and they gave us all a lecture and they never even noticed that Caroline had a bun in the oven, the stupid eejits. What sort of doctor doesn't notice a thing like that? I mean, even old Beano worked that out. He told Samantha about it last night, she said, after he came round. He was in this pub, right, this is what he said to Sam, now, so I don't know how true it is, but I suppose it half explains things. Anyway, this mate he was with, his girlfriend is up the pole, and he – Beano's mate, I mean, the girlfriend's boyfriend, if you see what I mean – he's all into it, all excited about being a da, see, and he's telling Beano all about his girlfriend's symptoms, how her face got puffy and being sick and all, and suddenly, PING, he says, it hit him about Caro, that she must be pregnant, and he just saw red, he said, because she hadn't told him about it or nothing, so he came racing home, right, and then he found the place full of people, *his* place, the way he sees it, and I suppose it is really, he *was* here first. We were all lying around the floor, I mean, we *were* spaced out of our heads and all, and of course that made him worse, he said, even madder he got, and that's how he went for Caro, see. I dunno, now, I think maybe he just told it all to

Sam that way to try to make her feel sorry for him or something, but anyway, that's the story, according to him.

The main thing was, though, we got Caro out of the hospital without them wanting to sign her into the Rotunda or whatever, so she's happy enough about that.

[FADE OUT]

PART 3

from peril and
from woe

FADE IN

EXTERIOR: LARGE RAMBLY HOUSE – DAYTIME

No action at first, HOLD view of house, which is an
old grey institutional building, in its own grounds,
with outbuildings, some of them semi-derelict.
Then MOVE into the house, along a long, dark, tiled
corridor, and into a small bedroom, where WE SEE
Caroline, sitting on a bed, her legs drawn up under
her chin. She is staring out of the window.

She doesn't appear to be speaking, but gradually
we become aware of her voice, as if we are
overhearing her thoughts. MOVE slowly around the
room, and then finally CLOSE-UP on Caroline, now
visibly speaking TO CAMERA.

Caroline

Well, we couldn't stay, we couldn't stay after that, could
we? That's ... what Samantha reckoned anyway, in case,

well, in case … Beano came back. Mind you, he made himself scarce quick enough, done a, done a … runner first thing in the morning. Oh, Mr Big Guy, sure, Mr Cool Himself, strutting his stuff all over town, *swaggering* all over the place, throwing … shapes to beat the band, doing his, his, his … lousy hole-in-corner deals, nudge-nudge, wink-wink, show us the colour of yer money and all the rest of it. And then he loses the head like that, just loses the head altogether, and, and, and … goes for me with a *Stanley* knife. I mean, for God's sake, what sort of a sodding creep goes around with a friggin' Stanley knife in his top pocket? *Looking* for trouble that is, just looking for it, isn't it?

I can't … I really can't imagine, I can't think … why I ever, ever fell for him in the first place ... apart from him being quite good-looking, he is dead good-looking, isn't he? I suppose I just wanted … I just wanted to have *some-body*. It was fine for a while, in the beginning, wasn't it? I mean, I mean … he was sort of protective and every-thing, just when I was really at my lowest after all that stuff with my ma. And he is real tall and sort of hand-some, isn't he? But I'm sorry now, I really am, the state of me.

Anyway, he kept … he kept … he kept saying it wasn't his bleedin' baby. (That just shows how stupid he is really, Mr Clever Clogs, how can he *possibly* think he can know a thing like that?) What sort of a slut was I, he said, oh God, having a baby that wasn't his, he said. The nerve of him, calling me a slut. He's a pimp, he is, which is worse, isn't it? And a pusher, too.

So I said, I said, I said … I hoped it *wasn't* his … and that's true, it's true, I really do wish it wasn't, I'd rather, I'd rather … it had *no* da than that it had *him* for a da, the pig. I'd nearly rather not have it at all, if he's its da, that's what I thought before, for a while anyway, but sure what can you do? You can't blame the baby for who its da is, can you? And then, and then … when he went for me like that … and, and, I thought for sure, for sure I was going to lose it, then I realised … well, I didn't want to lose it, did I? It's my baby, isn't it?

It's funny, when you start thinking like that, when you say the word 'baby' to yourself, suddenly … well, suddenly it hits you … it's for real. That's scary, that is, real scary … that's when I wish, I really wish I had my ma. I mean, you realise it's not … well, it's not just being sick and goose-pimply and feeling as if you're made of lead and feeling shit-scared – it's an actual baby that is going to be *born* and cry and smile and drink its bottle and learn to walk and talk and it is going to be *mine* … my closest relation, my very own little daughter – or son, I suppose – you can't send it back if it's a boy, after all, can you?

I never thought of it that way before, about it being my blood relation – since my ma and da, well, there's only been … only been me, but now, well, now there's going to be *us* again, that's really … really it's great, isn't it?

Beano and me, for a while … for a while, I thought … well, I must've been very stupid, because I really thought we could be an 'us'. It was great, it was, having somebody … it was like a romance that you'd read about … you know, like in a book.

You know, gear is a bit like love. It's great, well, it is ... it's great in the beginning, like a big romance ... it's fabulous in the beginning, and in the beginning you don't know where ... where the love stops and the gear starts, you can't, you can't, you can't tell one from the other, because it's all this big ... big, marvellous, golden cloud, and you want to wrap yourself up in it forever and just feel great, great.

Only you don't feel great forever. You have to come down. Just like love, it is.

I haven't got ... well, I haven't got any brothers or sisters or nothing. Looking back on it, looking back, it made us very close ... me and my ma and da ... especially when I was very small, very small, it was like I was sort of, well, sort of a part of them really, just an extra bit added on, as if we were not really a family, just sort of a couple and a half, know what I mean?

I did sometimes ... sometimes, I really did wish I had ... a sister, a little sister ... when I was small, but even so, I was never really into babies much, I'd never have *decided* to have one ... but now that it's going to happen, well, it's different, isn't it? I mean, I'm stuck with it, more or less, so I have to make the best of it, haven't I?

Beano didn't see it that way, he didn't. He wanted me ... the bastard, he wanted me to get *rid* of it. That's ... that's what he said that time, just before he attacked me. 'Get rid of it, Caro, it'll have no life, just get rid of it, and we can go back to the way we were before, just the two of us, and we'll say no more about it.' As if he was offering me some sort of a ... some sort of a *deal*, you know? Oh yeah, big deal, 'we'll say no more about it,' like he's doing me a *favour* or something, like *I* done something on *him*.

That was when I realised … I realised there was no way, absolutely no way I was going to get rid of it. As soon as he said it – it sounds so ugly doesn't it, even just the words, even just calling it 'it' is horrible, isn't it – I knew I couldn't do it, I just couldn't … that I had to keep it, because, well, because … it's all I've got left, it's, I mean, she (or he), she is the only person in the world … the only one in the whole world that belongs to me. Well, I mean, I have aunties and cousins and all, but this baby is the only really close, really close person to me, isn't it? Anyway, well, anyway, there's been enough dead people in my life, is how I look at it. I'd like somebody, just one person, just one, who's going to make a life for themselves, and who'll be with me, who'll be mine. Your ma's always your ma, no matter what, isn't she? Well, I'd like that to be me now, the person that somebody else is close to forever and ever and ever. I really would. I want to be somebody's ma. Like love. Like a really great love story.

I don't … I don't feel so sick any more, which is great, that really helps, great, isn't it? God, you really appreciate feeling well when you've been feeling scummy, I can tell you. I still get a bit weak sometimes, a bit weak, and there's some smells I can't stand, but at least I can, I can keep my food down, now, and that's something, isn't it? You have to make the most of it … make the most of it, and Samantha is going to help me with it, she promised.

She is a real pal, isn't she?

I didn't want … to leave … the place we were in, even after Beano knifed me and all there, I just didn't want, didn't want to go … I liked it there, and I had my mates, but Samantha, she said we better get out of it. I mean, it was a complete hole, really, a complete hole, freezing and filthy and all the rest of it, but at least … at least it had a roof – well, half of a roof anyway – and it was someplace … someplace of our own, our own, but Sam, she reckoned it wasn't safe for me after what Beano done. She thought he might come looking for me again … and it would be better if I wasn't there. That doesn't make much sense to me, because this is not that big of a town, and if he wants … if he really wants to find me, he will, but Sam said there is no point, no point at all in making it easy for him and I suppose … I suppose she is right, isn't she? Anyway, she said I would have to start going to the clinic and I'd have to have an address.

I said, 'But *this* is an address.' She said they might send somebody … send somebody out to visit … and then they'd know it was, well … derelict, and then we'd all be taken into care. Terrified of being taken into care, Samantha is. 'We're too old for care,' I said, but she said they'd think of some way. I don't think she's right about that, she can't be, can she? Once you're too old for it, they can't make you, can they?

But then she said the baby … the baby would get taken into care when it was born, so that made sense, obviously they could do that all right, couldn't they? Sam said I needed to be somewhere, somewhere …

respectable, and that's how we ended up here, me and Sam, in this terrible, cabbagey-smelling place, with the nuns – only they're not real nuns, I don't think, they wear these skirts and blouses, but anyway, they're very, very holy. So holy that they don't allow you to have boyfriends.

Can you *imag*ine, a place for grown women where you're not allowed to have a fella? I mean, well, I mean, they can't stop you having one, I suppose, but you're not allowed … you're not allowed to see them here. They aren't allowed in. If they need to see you, they have to … have to knock on the door, and you have to talk to them in the porch.

I mean, you can meet them outside, of course, but you can't at night because … because they lock the place up at ten o'clock. It's not that you aren't allowed out, it's not that, it's not that bad, but if you do go out, you see, you can't get back in again, can you? Once, once … they lock the doors, that's it for the night, the only fella you're likely to see after that is if there's a fire and the fire brigade comes out!

I don't mind … I couldn't care less if I never saw, if I never saw another fella in my life, but, well, it's hard on Sam, she's that fond of Curly. She misses him, misses him something dreadful.

Somebody said it was so that the … well, the violent husbands couldn't get in and start going for their wives … to keep us safe, like, and I suppose they're right about that, they are, aren't they? Still and all… still and all, I think it's really because these nunny people don't approve of sex. (Maybe they're right, because look what happens! Look at me.)

Anyway, Samantha said this is ... this is the best place for me now, because Beano, Beano can't get at me here ... and I have to admit it's nice to know I can go to sleep at night and he can't ... he can't come bursting in like he done the night of Johnner's party, can he?

Johnner, I was nearly forgetting about him, poor little sausage. He was heartbroken ... heartbroken he was ... about his party being ruined ... and about us, well, about us leaving and all. He loves that place, you know, you'd think it was a palace (I never told him, never told him about the rat, that'd have killed him), and he had it all ... all done up, with all these soccer posters that he brung from his ma's place and everything. He used to call it 'home', didn't he?

I couldn't ... I just couldn't think of it like that. When I think of home, it's me and my ma and da, before ... before he got sick, just the three of us, all together, like a family in a TV show ... with my da going out to work ... and my ma doing the cooking and cleaning and wearing an apron and all ... and me, me going to school. It was all so *normal* then, mammy, daddy, little girl, the way it is supposed to be, isn't it? We were a good family, weren't we? We were nice to each other. That's what makes it so ... so ... so sad.

I wish, I wish ... I wish I could have it back that way. It's not fair, is it? I mean, for one of them to die on me is bad enough, but why, why did the *two* of them have to get it? It makes you wonder is there something in the air or what? Makes me think … well, makes me think sometimes I'm going to get it, too. It's not fair on one person to have all the bad luck, is it?

But maybe, well, maybe I'll have a fresh start now with this baby. Maybe that will be the end of all the bad luck, mightn't it? I hope so, and I hope it's a girl. Girls are … nicer, and they can't grow up into their da, can they?

[CUT TO –]

INTERIOR: THE SQUAT – DAYTIME

Johnner

I do miss them all something terrible, I do. I know that sounds stupid, we were only all together about six weeks, but it was, like, the only place I ever felt at home in, like a kind of family, yeah. No disrespect to my ma now or anything, no way, but where I lived before, I mean, with them, my ma and da and all, I was only *living* there, it was just someplace, like, to *be* and there was always the oul' fella there, hanging over me like a threat, like a thunder cloud, big and black, he was, and you never know when it's going to burst. I mean, you couldn't rest easy in an atmosphere like that, know what I mean?

Even when I was small, I mean. He used to keep, like, a bamboo cane. In those days we had, like, a Sacred Heart picture that my nana gave my ma for a wedding present (I won't repeat the things my da used to say about that), and he used to, like, hang the cane on the Sacred Heart picture hook, so that you could see the crook of it sticking up behind yer man's head, like. All he had to do was, like, look at it, just cock an eyebrow at it, and I'd be shivering, yeah.

That's what I think about when I, like, think about that flat, *shivering* at the thought of what my da was going to do next. That was before he started, like, drinking. He got worse then, except that he didn't bother with the cane any more, he just hit you with, like, his fists. Sometimes he would get you out of bed to be beaten. I mean, you'd be *asleep*, for God's sake, how could you possibly be doing anything wrong in your sleep? But he'd come in drunk, yeah, and he'd haul you out of bed in your, like, pyjamas and start knocking you about.

I used to pee the bed. I mean, not usually, but when I'd hear him coming for me, like, I couldn't help it, and of course that gave him an excuse, he'd pull down the blankets, and I'd be lying in it, all wet and steaming, like, and at the same time starting to get cold already, and the smell rising up – it always smells worse when you do it in the bed, I don't know why – and he'd start roaring, 'Here's the lad that's too lazy to go as far as the friggin' toilet. Get out of that, you young pup you.' And he'd pull you out of the bed and start, like, punching.

He never touched my ma, no way. He had, like, funny ideas about that. 'I've never hit a woman,' he used to say, 'and I never will.' As if he was the great fella, you know. But he'd hit us instead, yeah, and not just because we annoyed him, I think he really done it to get at her, he'd hit me and my brothers – not the girls, they counted as, like, women, I suppose.

Ma'd cry and cry, yeah, and she'd, like, beg him to stop. I told her one day not to cry, not to take no notice, because that's why he did it, he did it to make her cry. That made her cry too, but she must've known I was right, because she never cried again when any of us was hit, and he, like, stopped after that. I mean, he still hit us, but only when he was, like, riled with us, he stopped making a production out of it, yeah, just to make her cry, because it wasn't, like, working any more.

She'd look at the wall, Ma would, and she used to, like, *sing*. That would drive him mad altogether, yeah, but he'd stop at us then and he'd go over to her and try to make her, like, stop singing, but she wouldn't, yeah. Still he never hit her. That's funny, isn't it? But it's just as well, I don't know what I'd do to him if he did that.

'Jeez, Ma,' I said to her one day, 'how can you *sing* when he gets going?' and she said, 'I have to do something with the tears, and if I sing, that sort of soaks them up, absorbs them somehow, like a shock absorber.' I didn't really, like, follow that, but anyway, it worked for her, I suppose. I think really it distracted her, yeah, gave her something to concentrate on, like, that wasn't us getting beaten up.

She left him once. I was about, like, six. She got me and my two brothers and Lorraine, she was about fourteen (my other sister had left by then and gone to England) and she made us take our books out of our, like, schoolbags and put our clothes into them and she packed a shopping bag for herself, and we, like, left. He was out at work, yeah, or the pub or someplace. I remember that

101

she locked the door, yeah, and put the key in her pocket and then off we went.

We got, like, a bus to someplace on the south side, Rathmines I think maybe it was, and we stayed in this refuge place for, like, battered wives. I used to think that was funny, battered wives, like battered sausages or fish. I mean, I used to imagine all these women with, like, their coats and scarves on, covered in batter, all ready for a dip in the deep-fryer, yeah. Well, I was only about six, how was I supposed to know what battered wives meant?

She wasn't, like, battered, though, it was only us, but she told the people in this refuge place that she was, because she thought you *had* to be, like, a battered wife, to stay there, I mean. She made up this story about how he used to knock her around, yeah. God, I used to be, like, dead shocked to hear her telling lies – my ma with the Sacred Heart picture! But I never contradicted her. Not that she ever said I wasn't to say nothing, but I didn't all the same, yeah, I knew to keep my mouth shut. Still, I was sort of, like, shaken by it, that she'd say that when all along it was us that used to be beaten. I felt sort of cheated or something, yeah.

We all went back after a while, though, yeah. My da found out where we were and he came around and gave them all grief, like, the people that ran the place, yeah, shouting out on the street and calling us all and crying and everything, and saying he was, like, so sorry. This went on for, oh, it was probably only about three or four nights, yeah, but it felt like forever, we used to be under the blankets, me and my brothers, like, with our fingers in our ears, yeah, trying not to hear, and my ma would try her singing trick again.

Hymns she used to sing, yeah. I think they were the only songs she knew the words of. 'The Bells of the Angelus' she used to sing, 'O Mary, we crown thee with blossoms today', and another Mary one about Star of the Sea or something. I never learned hymns at school, like, except 'He's Got the Whole World in his Hands', and that isn't a proper hymn, not really, I mean, it's more like an ad for Coca-Cola or something. But my ma, she knows, like, all these hymns. The tunes are a bit whiney, yeah, but when you listen to the words, they're really dead beautiful. There's one that goes on about being thrown on life's tide and then it goes on about, like, save us from peril and from woe. I used to think it was 'pearl' and I couldn't see why you would want to be saved from pearl, like. But now I know it is from peril and from woe, and it makes me feel sort of spooky, it's so, like, beautiful, like poetry is supposed to be, yeah, only it isn't usually because it's all about, like, clouds and daffodils and ploughing the fields and all this mucky culchie stuff, yeah.

Anyway, she sang all her hymns to the wall, my ma did, to the wall in the bedroom in that refuge in Rathmines, all these poetry words about, like, crowns and blossoms-the-rarest and hillside-and-dale and pray-for-the-wanderer and in-sweet-tones-announcing and save-us-from-peril-and-from-woe and when-wicked-men-blaspheme-thee and all, and he went on, like, roaring outside, John-ner, Dan-ny, Jiminy Crick-et. That was my brother Jim, we used to call him Jiminy Cricket just for fun, we did, like a pet name, but only in the house, yeah, he was mortified to hear it being shouted out on the street.

'Go out to him, Ma,' he used to beg her. 'Please go out to him and make him stop calling me that. I'm scarlet.'

In the end, anyway, she went out to him, yeah. She promised she would go home with him if he would stop disgracing us all on the street and if he would, like, promise to stop hitting us, and he said of course he wouldn't hit us ever again, yeah, and that he loved us all and he missed us. I could hear all this from the bedroom and I mean that was even more embarrassing than the hymns and the roaring, my da shouting out that he loved us. God, it was awful, it was.

So then we all packed up our schoolbags and we went home, but it wasn't because my da was going to stop hitting us, we knew he wasn't, yeah, it was because we had to share our bedroom with a family of knackers that had, like, nits, and my ma couldn't bear it any longer.

Knackers, that's what she called them, though I thought they were nice enough, yeah, once you got used to the way they talked, very country. Only there was millions of them, yeah, and there wasn't enough room. I don't think they, like, *really* had nits. I think my ma must've imagined it, probably, but once you start thinking about that sort of thing you can't stop, yeah, and you get all scratchy and you start, like, *dreaming* about things crawling over you, horrible it is, so that is the main reason we went back.

We never left him again. She sort of, like, lost heart after that. That's why I had to go myself in the end, I mean, because I knew she'd never leave again, and I figured out that if I was gone (I was the only one left by then), then things would probably be okay for her again, because it was only us he ever beat up on, and if we weren't there, like, then maybe there wouldn't be any more trouble, maybe they could just, I mean, get on with it and sort things out between themselves, yeah.

So anyway, here we are, Curly and me. But it's not the same with just the two of us. The crack isn't as good, though old Curly is, like, a great mate, he really is, but you miss the woman's touch about the place, I suppose.

I was so happy at first, just the freedom of it all, I suppose. It was, like, so great to be out of it, away from him, my da, I mean, and I really thought I could make something of this gaff, make it, like, a place that people really wanted to be in, but that's all over now, yeah. Beano stuck his, like, stupid big fist and his nasty little Stanley knife right through that idea, he did. I suppose it was a bit of a dream really, but it was, like, *my* dream, yeah, and he didn't need to mess it up like that, did he?

He done a runner, anyway, as soon as he, like, realised the amount of trouble he'd created. The rest of them stuck around for a bit, but that's when it, like, all started to fall apart, Beano pegging it that night. Sam said she had to get Caroline to, like, someplace better, that it wasn't good for her and the baby to be living in a squat. (I hate that word, 'squat', makes it sound as if we were sort of hunkering down, doing something dirty.) Sam said she would have to go with her, to one of them, like, hostel places, because I mean Caro needed to be minded. I could see that, yeah. I mean, poor old Caro, she couldn't cope on her own, but it was a bit rough on old Curly, all the same, I thought, they're only together a few weeks, and here's his mot, like, walking out on him, and he done nothing on her.

[CUT TO –]

Curly

I had a fierce row with Samantha, see. She won, of course. She always does. Stands to reason, she's smarter than me, that's why. It was bad enough her going off with Caroline like that, right. I mean, I do understand, I know Caroline is in a bad way and everything, but she didn't even *ask* me, she just said she was going, right, and then she starts giving orders before she goes. She said I was to stick with my Youthreach course. I told her where to get off. I said it was none of her bleedin' business what I did, and she said it *was* her business, and I said it wasn't, and she said it was, and then I just sulked, because I couldn't think of any way of making her see that it wasn't, see. That's me, see, I'm not good at the arguing, because I can't think of the answers fast enough, while it's happening, right. I dunno why, because I can think of them after, but it's no good thinking of them afterwards.

So then she said she was sorry, right, and she said I was a saint to be doing my course at all, considering everything. She said it would be a crime to give it up now, see. I said I wasn't going to stay on it, I couldn't see the point in it any more, stands to reason. But she said you have to see things through, and anyway if I didn't do it, I would be worse off.

So then I said I didn't *care* if I was worse off, right, and I said that I was fed up with her for going off and I just didn't want to be bothered. But then she said that if I didn't stick with it, she wouldn't see me any more. (She has a nerve really, when you think about it. She wouldn't go near a course with a barge-pole herself, scared she is, scared of teachers and classrooms and people being in charge of her, says she can't stand it. Gets real upset if you even mention the idea. She has a fierce temper, has Sam, when you hit on one of her sore spots, see.) So I said that she was leaving me anyway, that's how I seen it, so it didn't make any odds, but she said she wasn't leaving me, she was just going with Caro, see.

'Same difference,' I said, 'leaving, going, where's the distinction?' I thought that was pretty brainy of me, to think of putting it that way, but she's too fast for me. Always has an answer, has Samantha.

She said it wasn't a difference between leaving and going, it was, now let me see if I can remember this, because it's a bit complicated, she said it was a difference between *leaving* a person and going *with* a person. She said she wasn't leaving *me*, just going *with* Caro. Right.

'Oh, so she's your girlfriend now, is that it?' I said. 'You're going with her?' What a stupid thing to say! I dunno. I didn't mean that at all, right, but anyway she didn't take offence, because she knew I was just all cut up, and I was, I really was, right, so she said I could come and see her and she would see me, but I must keep on doing my course. So in the end I said I would, see, and I am.

I know, I'm an awful eejit to be letting a young one tell me what to do, but that's me. She has this idea that we have to 'better' ourselves, see. I think she's living in a dream there, but still, it's better than just dossing around all the time, and I am learning stuff on the course, right, and anyway, I don't want her breaking up with me, I really don't, so I'm sticking with it for the moment.

I never had a girlfriend before, see. I dunno, I thought I never would have, because I'm sort of slow off the mark with girls, that's the way I look at it. The other fellas always got in before me, right. But it was different with Sam. We, oh, we sort of clicked from the beginning. She was pals with this girl Sally, see, the one that gave her the platform sandals that she's so proud of, and they were having a drink one night, the pair of them, sharing a can in the park, and I was hanging around with this bloke that knows Sally, he lives near her, and so we all got talking, and Sam passes me over the can, right, so I can have a drink. I thought that was dead-on, but I said no, I didn't want any, because there was only one can and there was four of us, right, but anyway, she starts saying if I don't drink I must be very good-living and healthy and all the rest of it. I thought she was taking the piss, I dunno, teasing me for not taking a drink, but she wasn't, she was just talking, for something to say, and suddenly it dawned on me, right, that a *girl* was actually talking to me, taking the time to have a conversation with me, and I felt great, right, and then I realised that when this happens, you have to talk back, that's how it works, see, I didn't really know that before, see, because I can be a bit shy sometimes, and if anyone talked to me that I didn't know, I really wouldn't talk back much, but this time, I just knew I had to keep talking, and I did. The two girls had the can finished, but they went on talking to the pair of us, and then it started getting cold, so we said we would go for a walk to warm up a bit, and in the end, we all went back to this gaff where Sam was staying with Caroline and Beano, and they had another can or two back there, so we stayed on, and then Sally, she started getting worried about going home, right, because her mother kills her if she is out too late, so the bloke that was with me, Jason was his name, he went off with her to help her face up to the ma, he knows her oul' one well, he grew up in the same flats, see, and I just sort of stayed on, and me and Sam talked all night, we just talked and talked and talked, right. I asked her why she wasn't going home, and she said she hadn't got a home, that she was out of care, and she had nowhere, so she was staying with Caroline, but she wouldn't talk about growing up in care, she is real touchy about that, only I noticed these scars on her wrists, and I thought, Jeez, she's had a rough time of it, right, and I thought she could do with somebody to look after her, only she thinks *she's* the one that's looking after me. So that's why I was so upset, see, when she walks out on me and goes off with Caroline, because we were just getting real close, me and Sam.

I tried to get Johnner to do the Youthreach, too. I got one of the teachers to talk to him, right. There's one real nice teacher on it, young and all, and me and her get on great, she helps me with stuff, see, and I can talk to her, you know, like just talking to a person, not a teacher, right. So I asked her if she'd have a word with Johnner and she did, but I dunno, it turns out he's too young to be on it, he'll have to wait. I think that's stupid, that's the way I look at it. Linda said that too – that's her name, this teacher, Linda, nice name that, sort of pretty, it suits her, she has blond hair, cut short, but with curly bits around her ears.

'But you can't buck the system, Curly,' she said, 'that's just the way it is.'

If any other teacher said a thing like 'buck the system', you'd think they were trying to be trendy, right, come down to your level, like, but when Linda says it, that's just the way she talks, see. She smokes too, the only one of them that does. The rest of them are such walking saints, right, that they don't even smoke, or not in front of us they don't anyway. That's stupid too, not smoking in front of us in case we might get the message that it's okay to smoke, and there *we* all are smoking in front of *them*, really sad that is, isn't it? That's the way I look at it, anyway.

I still feel bad about Samantha going off like that. I miss her and everything, but that's not what I mean, see.

What I mean is, it worries me that she had to make a choice between Caroline and me and she chose Caroline, see. But when I say that to Samantha she says it's not like that. It's not that she *prefers* Caro to me, right, it's just that Caro needs somebody just now, see. I dunno, though. I need her too, and I told her that. That's the way I look at it, anyway.

'Yeah, but you're not pregnant, are you?' she said.

Oh well, great, top marks for observation, right.

'Sex discrimination that is,' I told her. That's what I said, sex discrimination, that's the way I look at it. 'Seems the only way a person can get you to be with them is to get pregnant, and that cuts out half the human race. Us fellas haven't a chance, have we?'

She told me not to be stupid, right, and that made me mad, because, like I explained before, I am not stupid, and I am very, very tired of people calling me that, see.

But anyway, we have to get used to it. That's what I do say to young Johnner, we just have to get used to it. I dunno, I think that young fella's depressed, though, that's the way I see it. He's gone all quiet and he's lost that bounce he used to have, the way he used to get all wound up about things, see.

He says he misses the others. 'Beano?' I asked him. 'Do you miss Beano?' He laughed at that, and he said no, it was the girls he missed.

'I do, too,' I said.

I do, too.

[PAUSE then CUT TO –]

111

INTERIOR: THE HOSTEL – EVENING

Samantha is sitting on the floor by her bed, her feet straight out in front of her. She speaks TO CAMERA.

Samantha

It's okay here really, so it is. I mean, it's not what you would call nice, but in fairness, it's a lot warmer than that place we were with the lads, and they give you your dinner if you want it, and we have proper beds instead of just sleeping bags, so we do. One of the people here, her name is Maureen, I think, she said Caroline could go to a mother-and-baby home. I asked her if I could go with her, but she said no, it's just for mothers, but I could visit if I want, so I could.

I'd be worried about Caroline going there by herself, so I would, but Maureen, she says it's lovely, only two to a room, and when your baby is born, a room of your own for a while, and you can stay on for a few months afterwards, so you can. Anyway, she can't go yet, you have to be nearer your time, so we don't need to decide for a while. And then again, anything could happen between now and then, I always say, and that's a fact.

[PAUSE]

Me and Caroline went shopping the other day, so we did. I mean, we haven't got any money, but we went looking. I made her get all dolled up, so I did. She's been letting herself go a bit, you know, doesn't even bother to brush her hair some days, and that's not like her, she's always so well turned out, but now she sort of slops around the place in an old tracksuit, so she does. So anyway, I said she had to have a shower before we could go to town. You can't have a shower in the hostel, so you can't, it's too old-fashioned, that's the long and the short of it, they only have baths. So she said she would see if there was enough hot water for a bath. She went and felt the immersion and it was medium hot, hot enough anyway for a bath, but then again, when she got to the bathroom the bath was full of some woman's washing that she'd left steeping. I swear to God, there's always something, so there is. I mean, now, you couldn't just dump it, in fairness, because it would make the floor all wet, so it would, and there weren't any basins or anything to put it in.

There is this other bathroom, but then again, that one has a toilet in it, and there is just no point in trying to have a bath in it, so there isn't, because somebody always wants to come in and use the jacks and I swear to God, you get no peace in it. Afterwards, I thought that we could've moved the washing into the *other* bath, and used the bath in the bathroom *without* the toilet, but anyway, you'd still have had to carry all these cold, heavy, wet clothes, and it would still have made a mess, so it wouldn't have been worth the hassle, and that's a fact.

I said to Caroline that I'd bring her to the place I go to that has the showers, the day centre place. She didn't want to come, so she didn't, because she says it's for homeless people. I asked her what she thought we were.

'I'm not homeless,' says she. 'I have a home.'

'Where?' I asked her.

'Where I used to live,' says she, 'my ma and da's place.'

'Caroline, they're both dead, lovey,' says I. I swear to God, I was beginning to think maybe being pregnant had made her soft in the head, so I did.

'I know, but that's my home,' she said.

I didn't push it. She never talks about her ma and da being dead, and I didn't want to upset her, so I didn't, not in her condition – she's kind of fragile, so she is, at the moment. I don't mean just that she's pregnant, I mean, she's kind of edgy-like and sort of distracted. I swear, I thought for a while that maybe she has this mad idea that the flat is still there waiting for her. But she couldn't think that, because if she really did, she would've tried to go there and live in it. I mean, we could've moved in, the pair of us, instead of living in this *convent*. Curly could be there too, even. That'd be nice, wouldn't it? (Ah, I'm getting as bad as Johnner, now, so I am, trying to stick everything back together, even though it's all broken apart.)

I think she just means that that is her home in her head. But I suppose that is better than no home at all, like me. The stupid thing is, my ma and da are out there somewhere, and my brothers, too, they didn't go into care at all, I don't know why, so in a way, I *could* have a home if I really looked for them, but I don't want to. I'm never going back to them. The drink is their family now. I was only eight when I was put into care, so I was, and they only came to see me on my birthday, and half the time they'd be drunk anyway, so when I was ten, I decided I was never going back to them again, never. I was only ten, but fair play, I knew they were no good for me, and I was right, so I was. I'm better off.

Anyway, no matter how many homes you have in your head, it's no good when you want a hot shower and there's no place to have it except a homeless place, so I got her to come with me in the end. We had a lovely shower, so we did. It's amazing how good it makes you feel, isn't it? I saw Caro getting out of the shower, before she put her towel around her, so I did, and she has this little fat place on her stomach, you couldn't call it exactly a bump like a really pregnant person, it's more a little cushion of fat, and that was the first time I really thought 'baby', when I looked at her, so it was. Usually I think, 'Is she eating enough vegetables?' or, 'Is it too late to start taking folic acid?' (I saw this programme about folic acid and it really would make you think, and that's a fact), but when I saw that little cushion of fat I thought, 'She's going to have a *baby*,' and I wondered if it would be a boy or a girl and what we're, I mean, what *she's* going to call it. It's amazing how it gets to you, so it is.

After that I took her to another homeless place, a kind of café it is, and she said it was okay, she said the scones were nice, and it was okay to sit in, but that was because the homeless people weren't there that day. I said they were. 'Look at them, all around you,' says I. She said they weren't homeless people. I said, 'No, they're not, just like you're not, Caro,' and she gave me this funny look, so she did.

Anyway, after that, we went shopping. We went to Penneys and Clerys, so we did, and Arnotts and Dunnes and Roches and Marks and Debenhams, and everywhere we went we looked at baby clothes, it was great. I couldn't get over them. I mean, I never really looked properly at baby clothes before, not ones for very tiny babies anyway, and that's a fact. Sure I never had any reason to. They were like little dolly clothes, so they were. I couldn't really believe that a real human being could possibly fit into any of them. We had a right laugh over them, picking up these little tiny vests and holding them up and trying to imagine little arms in them. They have these really gorgeous ones, dead soft, beautiful they are. You don't have to put them over their head; they're like little waistcoats, so they are, and they tie at the side with white satin ribbons, so they do. Can you imagine somebody thinking that up, little tiny vests tied together with satin ribbons?

Another thing they have is Babygros with little built-in mittens, can you believe it? It's to stop them scratching their little faces with their fingernails, so it is. I never knew they did that, but when you think about it, it must be murder trying to cut a baby's fingernails. I remember hearing about women biting their baby's nails, because it is easier than cutting them, but I swear to God, that sounds sort of barbaric to me, like being a cannibal or something, it's nearly as bad as eating the afterbirth, which they do in some countries, believe me (I saw a programme about that too – we used to watch a lot of telly in the home).

Caroline got a bit depressed looking at all these baby things, so she did, especially when she looked at the prices. 'They're only supposed to last for three months,' says she, 'look, it says on the label "nought to three months," and then you have to go out and buy them all all over again.'

I said, well, you could go to the Oxfam shop or the Simon shop, and she said she didn't think they'd have them little vests with the ribbons in the Oxfam shop, so they wouldn't, only old washed-out Babygros, all bobbly with wear and sort of stiff and hard from all the washing powder. That's probably true, but then again, I said, maybe you could get enough together for the first three months and maybe you could switch to the Oxfam shop later, like, when the baby's skin would be a bit tougher, so it would, and it mightn't mind a few bobbles. That didn't make much impression on her, so it didn't.

'It's going to cost a *fortune*,' says she.

'Yeah, but there's your money, you know, for unmarried mothers,' says I, 'single parents, I mean.'

That cheered her up no end. She'd forgotten about that, so she had, if she ever even knew about it.

'Hey, yeah,' says she. 'Free money! How much is it?'

Not enough probably, when you think of all the stuff you have to get when you have a baby, but I didn't say that. She doesn't need to think about that yet, no point in depressing her, it's bad enough as it is.

'It must be a fair bit,' says she then, 'because they don't want people having abortions.'

'*What*?' says I. I couldn't believe my ears, so I couldn't.

'No, it's true,' she said. 'I heard them going on about it on the radio one time. Something about cherishing life and that sort of rubbage.'

'So you mean, they *bribe* you to keep your baby?' says I.

'Yeah, stupid isn't it?'

It isn't really stupid, when you think about it, so it isn't, but anyway, I didn't believe her. I just laughed. Sometimes I think she's a bit innocent, Caroline, even with all her experience. But then I thought, God, maybe that's what she's thinking of doing, you know, going to England, so I asked her if she had ever, you know, considered it, and she went pure mad, she nearly scratched my eyes out, so she did, for even *mentioning* it.

'This is *my baby* we're talking about, Sam, not some … some … some *foetus*.' And I swear to God, she was sobbing that much, she was stuttering, it took her real bad it did, I was sorry I'd said anything, I just thought maybe she wanted to talk about it, so I did, when she brought the subject up, I mean, I wasn't the first one to mention it. 'I may be a tart,' she said then, 'but I'm not a murderer as well.'

'Tart?' says I. 'Oh Caro, you're not a tart, I never said you were a tart, getting pregnant doesn't make you a tart. Anyway, it's not murder, it's not the same.'

'It is,' says she, 'it's the very same,' and she was roaring crying. 'What's the difference?' says she to me. 'Tell me, what's the difference?'

Well, I wasn't going to argue with her, was I? I'm not

the one that has to have the baby, but I mean, look at all the miscarriages that women have, it happens all the time, that's just nature, isn't it? Don't get me wrong, I don't think it's a great idea, I swear to God, I don't, I probably wouldn't want to do it myself, so I wouldn't, but still, oh God, I don't know, it's hard to know, isn't it? When you think about it, like. Anyway, it's not like I was *encouraging* her to do it or anything. I only wondered if she'd *considered* it, I didn't mean any harm, I was only *asking*, so I was.

It's mad really, because I *like* babies, so I do, I wouldn't want to do them any harm or anything like that, that's not what I mean at all. It's just that, when you think about all the years and years of bringing up a child, and sure we're only children ourselves, really, when it comes down to it, not much more more, anyway.

When I lived in the home, we used to have babies sometimes, so we did. It was mostly older kids, only a few young ones, and just now and then some little ones or maybe a baby. When we had a baby, I used to hang around with the care-workers, mad to be allowed to help, I was. They used to get real annoyed at me sometimes, so they did, for getting in their way, but when they realised I really did like babies, genuine like, they would let me do things, like they'd let me get the nappies or put the Babygros to air in the hot-press, they even let me sterilise the bottles sometimes, which is not a very interesting job, so it isn't, because you don't get to touch their little clothes or anything, but at least you are doing something useful.

Anyway, when we got back to the hostel, I gave Caro the three-pack of vests that I'd robbed, so I did, the ones with the little satin ribbons. You could've knocked her over with a feather. She never even saw me, and she was with me the whole time, so she was. I'm good at knocking stuff off, I've loads of practice, so I have. She started crying again when she saw them, and she gave me this wet, slobbery kiss. Soppy, isn't it? You'd swear I'd *knit* them or something. I swear to God, I think it's the hormones, they take some people that way.

'God, Sam, thanks,' says she.

'That's okay,' says I, 'any time.'

I'm going to build up a trousseau for that baby. (I think that's what you call it – or is it a bassinet?) There'll be no Oxfam stuff for this one, so there won't! Maybe Caro'll ask me to be godmother, God, that'd be great, that'd be deadly, if she has a christening. Then again, I suppose she mightn't. I mean, she's not exactly religious, but you could still have a sort of honorary godmother, couldn't you? Though, then again, she mightn't after what I said about going to England. She probably thinks I'm some sort of a monster, that I have something against babies or something. God, I was only *asking*.

One thing about having a baby is that it's easier to get a flat, so it is. I mean, some people think girls have babies just to get a flat. I swear to God, they must be off their rocker. Have a *baby* just for that? Sign away the whole rest of your life? I don't think so. But still, if you are going to have a baby, you might as well try for a place. With two kids it's nearly definite you'd get a place, but one is better than nothing, so it is. I said to Caroline she should put her name down immediately, and she might be lucky, and then, if she likes – only if she likes, of course – I could move in with her for a while, so I could, to help her with the baby. I was telling her about how experienced I am and everything with babies, and she was laughing at me, telling me she'd be needing a nanny, but she'd need good references and all. I mean, I know she was joking, but she is going to need someone to help her, so she is, and she only has me, and that's a fact. That's all. Makes you feel very responsible, so it does.

[PAUSE]

You know, it's funny, things have turned around a bit, because it was Caroline that began by looking after me, so it was. I met her one day in a bus shelter. She was waiting for a bus, I was just there for the shelter. It was soon after she'd shacked up in that squat place with Beano, so it was, and she was sort of walking on air, all in love and everything, she was like a bride, she was, her face was all beaming and it was nearly like she was shining with the joy of just being with him, you know. God, when you think about how all *that* changed so fast, and that's a fact.

She was waiting for a number 49, so she was, to go out to visit her auntie that she used to live with, to tell her she was okay, because she'd run away from home and then she'd met Beano, and the poor auntie didn't know where she was, and she thought she better go and tell her she was all right.

I wasn't long out of care, so I wasn't, and I didn't have any place, because I wouldn't go back to my ma and da, like I swore all along I wouldn't, so I was sleeping rough. It was the summertime, so it wasn't so bad, but this day it suddenly got cold, and I was just thinking I didn't really want to spend the night out. I was wondering if I should try to look for a place in a hostel or something, so I was, but the wind was so sharp I couldn't think, it was whipping around my head, it was, and I felt as if it was cutting into my brain. Then I saw this bus shelter, and says I to myself, if I just stand in there out of the wind, it won't be warm, but at least the wind won't be able to knife my brain, and I might be able to think, so I might.

Terrible upset I was that day, I remember, and lonely too, and just plain miserable I was. I think I must've sat for hours in that bus shelter, with my knees up against my chest, and I was trying to get a bit of heat into me, I was, and all these thoughts were going round and round in my head, so they were, at a fierce rate, all thoughts about the heap of shite that my life was, and I was thinking, well, I have to admit, I was thinking I was going to cut my wrists, so I was, and I was wondering where I could find a glass bottle to break, so I could do it. I used to do that, you know. I know, mad, isn't it, you wouldn't think it, but in them days, I swear to God, I was that sad and angry, I used to do it, just sometimes. Not deep, I mean, I wasn't trying to kill myself, so I wasn't. It's just that when you cut yourself, well, the blood and everything, and the pain, it's like … well, imagine if you are carrying this really heavy bucket, okay, and you are all bent over to one side, so you are, trying to carry it. Well now, that bucket is all the shit in your life, so it is, all the pain and the anger and the lonely feelings that you have, and you are aching and aching, trying to carry it, so you are, and then somebody comes along and they give you another bucket, so they do, and that bucket is dead heavy too, but you pick it up with your other hand, and for a little while, you have this mad idea that it's easier now, you can carry the two buckets easier than one, because now you're better balanced, so you are. You're still aching all over, but the ache is spread around more. Well, that's what it's like when you cut yourself, and that's the long and the short of it. The pain of the cut is like the second bucket. It sort of balances out the pain of your life, so it does, and for a little while, I swear to God, you think you can cope better with it all, so you do. It's a bit mad, I know, but at least it doesn't do anyone any harm, except yourself, and it costs nothing, and it doesn't make you pregnant or string you out. I mean, I'm not recom*mend*ing it, now, so I amn't, I'm just explaining, so I am.

So anyway, there I was, huddled up in the corner of the bus shelter and thinking about cutting my wrists and all, when this young one comes over and starts talking to me, so she does. I swear to God, I thought for sure she was some sort of an outreach worker or something, nicely dressed she was and all, so she was, and I was thinking up a story to tell her, so I was, so she might be able to get me a bed for the night, and the next thing she's telling me about sleeping in a haybarn out beyond Enfield, so she is. I never even heard of Enfield, so I didn't. I didn't know what she was on about, I swear to

God, I hadn't a clue, but in the end I worked out she was like me, and then she said she had a place with her fella and did I want to stay with them.

Well, obviously, I did. A godsend it was to me. I didn't cut my wrists that day, so I didn't, and I never done it from that day to this, and I always say I have Caroline to thank for that, and that's one reason why I have to stand by her now. I owe her, like.

Soon after that, anyway, I met Curly, and he moved in as well, so there we were, the four of us, and we got on grand for a while, so we did. Caroline says that when Johnner came along, things began to go wrong, but that's not fair really, you can't blame poor oul' Johnner. It was Beano was the trouble all along as far as I'm concerned, he didn't really want any of us there, so he didn't, and anyway it was him throwing a wobbly that night that broke it all up in the end, and that's a fact. But I didn't say any of this to her. I never mention Beano, so I don't. I mean, where's the point? He's not here, and he's worse than useless. He's dangerous, he is.

[CUT TO –]

INTERIOR: THE SQUAT – DAYTIME

Johnner is sitting on a sleeping bag, his head in his hands. HOLD for a BEAT, then Johnner looks up and starts to talk.

Johnner

I got a terrible shock, I did. Lorraine has had her babby. That wasn't the shock, though, I mean, we were expecting that. She was, like, ready to pop for ages, so when she finally did, we weren't exactly surprised. Another girl, it was. That's two girls now, and one young fella, yeah.

I minded her two kids for her when she was, like, in the hospital. Not all by myself, of course, no way. My ma came around to her place, she moved in for a few days, like, but I used to go around there every day to let Ma go out and do the bit of shopping, and drop over to Holles Street to see Lorraine. I'd get a bit of dinner there with them all, yeah, and then I'd help with the washing up, and then I'd stay around for a few hours when Ma went off, like, on business. That's what you say to Dawn and Jordan (that's Lorraine's kids) when you have to go out and they can't come, that you're going, like, on business. When they hear that, they know it means strictly no kids, yeah.

It was nice, it was being a proper uncle, you know, nearly like being a da, even, the sort of da *I* would be if I had chisellers, yeah. I played them, like, my United videos, all the best games. I can't watch them in my own gaff, of course, so I keep them over in Lorraino's, and I do watch them when I'm over there, yeah.

She tapes all the matches for me, does Lorraine, so I don't miss anything – she has, like, Sky Sport, with the decoder and all, Damien is big into football, he is, so he set it all up – and then I watch them all, and the really good ones I keep, and I do watch them over and over again, all the time, yeah. Only the ones we won, mind you. No point in depressing yourself, like, with stuff like that Southampton match, no way. The problem is,

Damien supports Arsenal, which I reckon is bad for them kids, so while he's not around, I try to get them, like, interested in the right team. It's part of their heritage. I mean, I'm their uncle, after all. I'm, like, saving my Cantona poster for Jordan when he's older, and I can give it to him, the way my uncle Ken gave me his Busby Babes poster, yeah, which *he* got off *his* uncle, my grand-uncle Mickser.

I have this United jersey, well actually, it's out of date, they're always, like, changing the strip, but anyway, *I* know it's United, yeah, and I wear it when I'm, like, watching the matches, and I get Dawn and Jordan to cheer when we score, I do. We do cheer and fling things in the air and if it's, like, a really special goal, and especially if it's Our Roy that scores (which, of course, it hardly ever is, it's usually one of the black fellas), well, anyway, if Roy Keane scores, we do a little dance around the couch, you should see us, like Indian braves doing a bleedin' war dance. They do love it, the kids. No, they do, really.

I suppose Damo will kill me when he gets home and finds his kids, like, cheering for United. That's what happens when you get put away, things go on without you, little things, things you mightn't notice if you were around all the time, but by the time you get back, things must feel different, you must really get the feeling that life has been going on without you, sort of behind your back, while you were inside.

Anyway, his kids growing up to be United supporters is only, like, the half of it. I can't imagine what Damo is going to say when he hears about *this* – if he does hear about it, that is, I'm certainly not telling him, no way.

It was visiting day in Wheatfield yesterday and Lorraine was home from the hospital and she had the new babby with her, Debonaire she wants to call her (I think she must've got that out of a storybook or off of a film or something). Anyway, she wanted to bring the child with her to visit Damien, let him see, like, his new daughter, and she didn't want to bring Dawn and Jordan with her, I mean, she couldn't manage them all on the bus, so I said I'd mind them for her. I said I'd be over after dinner time – you can't be always arriving in at mealtime, like, it's not fair on people – and I said I'd stay there until she got back, because my ma had, like, an appointment with the chiropodist and she couldn't do it.

Anyway, I was a bit late getting over to Lorraine's place, I was, and I was worried that she'd be getting edgy, like, and I thought to myself, oh well, she can always leave them in the flat and ask Stacy from the flat next door to keep an eye on them until I get there. There's no reason for her to, like, miss her bus. This is the way I was thinking, I was, and I legging it up the stairs to the flat. I was feeling a bit guilty, I suppose, because I was that bit late, and I arrived at her front door all out of breath, steaming I was. I had to stop at the top of the stairs for a good cough, because when I run, it all sorts of sticks in my chest, the snotty stuff, it does.

I knocked on the door, I did, because, like, I couldn't find my key, and I was just thinking that if she'd left the kids, Dawn wouldn't be able to reach the latch to let me in. Next thing, the door opened, just a crack, like. She must be here still, I thought. 'Sorry Lorraine, sorry I'm late, I got held up, here, you better make a dash for it or you'll miss the bus …'

Here I was going on all with all this story, yeah, and pushing the door to go in, only the door wasn't giving, no way, the person on the other side was, like, pushing back. It must be Dawn, I thought then, farting around, playing a game with me, so I didn't push too hard in case I hurt her.

Next thing, this head appears around the door and if it isn't Beano! When he seen it was me, he stopped messing about with the door and he let me in. Then he turned back into the room. He was doing something at the cooker, I couldn't see exactly.

'Hey, Beano,' I said, all nervy, like, well you can imagine, I mean the last time I saw this bloke he'd just cut up one of my best pals, yeah, 'what's the story?'

'StOhry?' he says, like that, with a big OH in the middle of it, 'stohry? There's no story, Jonathan.'

Jonathan! Where did he get that out of?

'Johnner,' I said, 'name's Johnner.'

'Oh yeah, sorry, Johnny,' he says, real insulting, like. That was deliberate that was, he was doing it on purpose, calling me out of my name, yeah.

I could see what he was at now, he had this, like, spoon, you know, a Cornflakes spoon, and he has something in it and he's sort of, like, cooking it over the gas ring.

'Eh, is Lorraine here?' I asked. I was wondering if she'd left him in charge of the kids. It wasn't like her, if she did.

He leant over the spoon and there's all smoke coming off it and he's sniffing it, practically *drinking* it in, he is.

'Lorraine?' he asked, sounding all vague, God, he must've been really strung out, yeah, he couldn't seem to remember whose place he was in, or else he was trying to get a rise out of me, he was.

'Yeah, Lorraine, my sister,' says I, 'she lives here.'

'Oh ye-ah,' he says then, dead cool and drawly. 'She's your sister, I was forgetting.' And he gives another big sniff, closing his eyes.

'Where is she? Has she taken the kids with her?'

I couldn't imagine Lorraino leaving her kids with Beano, no way, even if she was stuck for a babysitter. I mean, she knows what he's like, she was there the night he went for Caroline. She bandaged her up and all.

'Oh yeah,' he says, real slow, like, 'she's after taking them out.'

'To Wheatfield?' I said. 'Ah, no. She'll never be able to manage them all on the bus, not with the babby, no way.'

'Norra-tall,' says Beano, 'not gonnta Wheefeel. Gonnta po-soffice forrer money.'

It took me a while to work that out.

'Oh, right,' I said then, when I realised, like, what he was after saying, 'so she'll be back so before she goes. What are you doing here, Beano? I didn't know you were a friend of hers.'

'Frenn?' he says, and he guffaws out of him. 'I wouldn't say that ezzackly.' He's finished whatever he's at so he turns off the gas and he flings the spoon into the sink. Then he sat down on Lorraine's settee and put his feet up on the table, yeah.

It gave me, like, a dead creepy feeling, the way he was talking, but at least he was in a mellow mood, you know, he didn't look as if he was going to beat somebody up or go for them with a knife or anything like that. Still, I was a bit nervous, like, but, I mean, I put the kettle on and I washed the spoon – it was all sticky – and I waited for Lorraine to come back.

She was ages, I thought she'd never get there. I was making the tea real slow, like, trying to spin it out, so that I'd have something to do, like, so I wouldn't have to sit down and talk to Beano. I couldn't imagine myself saying, 'Well, Beano, so how's it goin'?' as if nothing had happened, but I couldn't imagine myself saying anything else either, and it would be, like, terrible embarrassing and tense just to sit there and say nothing at all.

Anyway, she got back at last, did Lorraine, with the youngsters, and they were all whinging, even the small one. I could hear them coming, so I went out to give her a hand, like, with the buggy up the steps. She had Jordan in the buggy and the baby in her arms, I don't know how she managed them all, and Dawn was dragging out of the handle of the buggy as well, yeah. We got them all inside, and Beano stood up as soon as he saw her and put his hand out.

At first, I thought he was offering to give her a hand

with the kids or something, but the next thing, Lorraine is giving him money, *wads* of money, like, and her book, the book for getting the money, you know, with the dockets in it, the vouchers, whatever you call them, for the children's allowance or whatever it is.

He counts the money, he does, he rolls it up and he puts it in his top pocket, cool as you like, and he hardly looks at the book, just puts it in his back pocket, yeah.

'Goodbye, sweetheart,' he says then, and I swear to God, he actually blows her a kiss. He kisses the tips of his fingers and then he blows on them, in her direction, gross it was, and next thing he, like, swings off out of the door and we can hear him clattering down the stairs outside.

Gobsmacked, I was, absolutely gobsmacked. I didn't dare to ask her what was going on, like. I could guess anyway. She owes him money (and I don't want to know why, I really don't) and he's making damn sure he gets it, all of it. I don't know how much he left her. I don't know if it's enough – well, it *can't* be enough, it's hardly enough as it is, without giving half of it to some bastard like Beano.

But he didn't have to take her book, like. If she owes him the money, she'll pay him, he doesn't need to keep the bleedin' book. It's not right that, it's just not right, I mean, he might lose it or anything and then where'd she be? Ah, God, it's awful. Poor Lorraine.

'Here, have a cuppa tea, Lorraine,' I said. She needed it. She was shaking. She was white. I mean, she's only out of the hospital.

I put extra sugar in it. That was the only thing I could think of to do for her, the only thing.

[CUT TO –]

Curly

I dunno, I never saw young Johnner in such a state. His face was streaked with crying, right, and his eyes looked sore. He tries to act the big fella, right, most of the time anyway, especially with me, he has this idea I'm dead tough, that's the way I see it, so it must've been bad for him to let down his guard like that and let me see that he'd been crying.

He's only a kid, see, he's too young to be living like this, and then worrying about his family into the bargain. I mean, I know what it's like to be worrying about your family. It doesn't matter what sort of a family it is, it doesn't matter if you couldn't get away fast enough from them, it doesn't matter if they treated you rotten when you were a kid and threw you out as soon as you started shaving – your ma is still your ma, and I suppose it must be the same with your sisters and brothers, if you have any.

Samantha doesn't agree with me about that. She swears she hates her family and never thinks about them from one end of the year to the next. I say hating them is thinking about them, but that just gets her mad at me.

I never see my ma now, but I don't hate her. I worry about her. She lives with this bloke that used to be married, and he has grandchildren, imagine, *grand*children.

But still, I do worry about her, I dunno, I worry about her living with a bloke with grandchildren. I don't know why that makes it worse, I just dunno. There's nothing wrong with grandfathers, I know that all right, but for some reason, I dunno why, it spooks me that he's one. There must be a reason for that, but I can't work it out, see. I will have to think about it very carefully, but, see, I haven't got time for thinking at the moment. She's only in her thirties, right, that's probably why it seems a bit weird. I mean, the grandchildren don't live with them or anything. It's just the *idea* of it, right.

And anyway, he doesn't like me, which is why I don't see her. I dunno, I think there is something funny about a bloke with grandchildren who keeps a mother from see-ing her son. Not that I put all the blame on him, ah no. I mean, if she really wanted to keep me with her, she could've, even if he didn't like it, right, but we've got out of touch by now anyway. Even if she wanted to see me now, she wouldn't know where to look.

But I know where she is. I like knowing that, see, even though I wouldn't go near her. I mean, I wouldn't create a scene. If she wants her grandfather bloke, she can have him. I'm not stopping her. I mean that, I don't think chil-dren should go messing up their parents' lives once they're old enough to look after themselves, see. That's the way I look at it.

But Johnner, he isn't old enough, see. He thinks he is, but he isn't – you can't tell him that, of course. I didn't know whether I should ask him straight out what was wrong, or if I should pretend I didn't notice, or what, it's hard to know, but again I looked at that thin little face all puffed up and pink, I had to say something, that's the way I look at it.

I tried to take it handy with him, not just say 'What's up, mate?' because I knew he'd freeze up if I said that, it's hard to know, isn't it? So instead I just sat down beside him on the sleeping bags – we have extra ones now, because the girls left us theirs, see, when they went off to that women's place they're in – and I said nothing for a long while. He sat staring off into space. He wasn't crying any more, he was just looking absolutely dismal, that's what I thought, anyway.

'Bugger it all,' I said after a while, not really to Johnner, half to myself, see. 'Life's a heap of dogshit, isn't it?'

He didn't answer, but his shoulders twitched a bit, right, so I knew he'd heard me. I had a can of lager, right, and I handed it to him for a slug, but he just shook his head, and I could see his nose curling up – he doesn't really like drink, not even the smell of it. I suppose it's minerals I should be offering him, a young fella like that. It's hard to know.

'I saw Beano today,' he said real suddenly, only he was still looking away from me. Then he started one of them coughing fits he gets, right. The damp here doesn't do him any good at all, that's the way I look at it. I think he has a chest infection. It sounds as if he has a coalmine down his throat, the amount of hoking and wheezing that he does be going on with.

'Beano!' I let a shout out of me. 'That hoor. Where is the bollocks till I smash him to pieces?'

Johnner only shrugged. 'He was at Lorraine's place,' he said then, real soft, like.

'Lorraine's?' says I. 'Your sister Lorraine's? The one that was here at the party?'

'Yeah,' says Johnner. 'Did I tell you she had her baby?'

'You did. Debonaire.' I let a bit of a laugh, right, to lighten things up, I mean, it's hard to know what to say, isn't it? 'I suppose they can call her Debbie and nobody need ever know,' says I. But Johnner didn't laugh.

Then he told me all about it, how Beano had took her book and was taking her money off her and all this story. God, I've heard it all a million times.

Then he says, all innocent like: 'You never think of moneylenders being young fellas like Beano, do you? I mean, they're usually these fat crooks, aren't they, these fellas in big limos and all, with suits.'

Moneylenders, that's what he thinks. Beano's no moneylender. He doesn't need to deal in money, right. He's got more interesting stuff in stock, that's how I look at it.

'No, eh, no, you're right,' I said. No point in making things worse for him, see, no point in rubbing his nose in it. 'Surprising, that is,' says I, all agreeable, like, 'yeah, surprising. Beano, who'd have thought it?'

But Johnner knows, he must know, that's how I look at it. He must know it's not moneylending that was going on between Lorraine and Beano. There was gear involved for sure – and her only home with the new baby, God help her. God, I hope it's for Damien – I mean, it's like gold dust inside, it could be for him – but I hope it's not for herself, not with all the small babies and all, ah God, no.

But Johnner, now – I *think* he knows, he *must* know, he couldn't be that innocent, he *lived* with the bloke for six weeks, he must know. Poor ould Johnner, you'd be sorry for him all the same. Poor Lorraine. And them poor babies – three she has now, I think. Ah God, it's not right. Really, it's not.

[FADE OUT]

PART 4

singing in the rain

FADE IN

INTERIOR: HOSTEL – EVENING

Caroline

You know, it's funny, well, funny isn't the right word ...
but, but, anyway, it's funny ... it's only since I got away
from him that I, that I really realise how terrible it was
living with Beano, wasn't it? You know, this probably
sounds, probably sounds, well, daft ... but when I, when I
... when I look back on it, I can see that I nearly *belonged* to
him there for a while ... the way, the way his jacket
belonged to him, or his package of cigarettes ... and I
probably meant about as much to him, which is the worst
part, really the worst, isn't it?

I wouldn't mind so much if I thought that I meant
something to him, even just, even just for a while.

I can just hear him, just hear him I can, delivering one
of his ... one of his fuckin' lectures: 'Everyone has something to sell, Caro, and that's really the basic method of

communication, if only people would face up to it and admit that that's how it all really works, when you get down to it.'

God, it was like a crusade with him ... a crusade ... he was like one of them religious freaks you see, you know, you see them on the top of ... the top of Grafton Street sometimes, the way he used to go preaching on ... preaching on about it, as if he was after finding the secret of life or something, when really what he's talking about ... he's talking about that ... that ... that lowlife dealing he does be going on with.

And he deals in anything, absolutely anything.

'I don't mean *things*, necessarily.' That's what he used to say, 'not necessarily.' He always was real pompous, a pompous rat, wasn't he?

'Some people can sell what's in their heads, people like me.' That's himself he was talking about ... Jamie Clancy ... aka Beano ... you'd think he was bloody well, bloody well Mary Robinson or someone. He's the bleedin' High Commissioner for Bullshit, he is.

'Take me, now, for instance ...' himself, he means, 'what I have to sell is what's in my head – when people buy off me, instead of buying off some other bloke, it's because they're really buying my business brain and my contacts and what I know and who I know and what I am able to do for them and what I can get for them.'

At the time, well, at the time of course, I didn't see it, just didn't, didn't see it. I was that glad to have some-body, to have someplace – I mean, I was so broken up, my da had died six months ago, and then my ma died two months after that, one after the other, I was devast ... dev ... just devastated, I was living under this big, black, angry cloud, well, that's what it felt like, I couldn't hardly eat or sleep, I couldn't hardly think, even. And then along comes this, this, this hunky fella, and he likes me and he's all *interested* in me and he's full of sympathy, and he *listens*, you know ... the first person that just listens, instead of telling me things like it's, it's, it's for the best and I should be glad, glad that they weren't suffering any more ... and that time is a great healer ... and I'll be able to put it all behind me any day, any day, any day now, and some day I'll have children of my own ... yeah, great, that's just, well, that's just terrific, isn't it, that really makes it all okay, doesn't it?

I was living with my auntie for a while, well, I moved in with her and her family after the, well ... after the funeral, my father's funeral, I mean. My ma was in hospital then, she wasn't even well enough, well enough to go ... to go to the funeral, and I went to live with Rosie, but she has all these, all these ... all these kids, I wasn't used to a big family, you know, and the noise was something awful and they were always fighting about who was going to watch what on the telly.

Rosie is dead-on, she done her best, but her kids are her kids, after all, and she has to be, well, she has to be their ma, hasn't she? She didn't really have enough left over for me, because I needed a ma *and* a da, plus I was in shock, in shock I was, plus I was so cut up about my da that I couldn't even visit my ma. Imagine that – my ma was dying, dying she was, and she wanted to see me and

I couldn't, I couldn't, I couldn't bring myself to go to her, could I? I mean, I went in the end, but she was in a coma by then and it was too late, too late, she didn't know I was there.

I let her down, didn't I? I know I did, let her down. And then she died on me too, and it was even worse than my da dying. You'd think, you'd ... well, you'd think, wouldn't you, you'd think it should've been easier, when I'd been through it before, but it wasn't, it was worse. It gets worse, not better.

God, I was real unhappy, all upset in myself. I wasn't able to do anything, I just wasn't *able*. I wasn't even able to cry. When I think back on it now, I was bullin', really in the horrors I was, snarling at them all all the time, throwing tantrums, banging doors, going missing for days at a time – I used to just walk out of the house, just walk out sometimes and just walk and walk and walk and I'd find I'd walked as far as Lucan or somewhere, and I'd keep on walking and when it got dark I'd just drop, just drop, any old place, under a tree or something (it was summertime, I remember) and sleep, or not really sleep, sort of doze off, in fits and starts, and then in the morning I'd get up and walk ... walk, walk again. I walked right into the country, I nearly got as far as Galway one time, didn't I? That was the time the guards ... well, they picked me up and drove me back to Rosie's, didn't they?

And all the time I had this pain ... this pain, this pain in my throat, not a sore throat, not like when you have a cold, just this really, well, this painful feeling, this ache that wouldn't go away. I went around for weeks with this aching ... aching throat. Sometimes it hurt so much that I couldn't even, couldn't even talk with it.

And then one evening, getting into September time it was, it was getting a bit late in the year for wandering off and sleeping in hedges – of course, it was time, well, it was time to go back to school, but I didn't even think about all that – anyway, there I was, not at school, sitting on a bench ... sitting, just sitting on a bench by the canal, well, just watching nothing much, a plastic bag, a plastic bag I think it was, caught in the branches of a tree overhead and flapping in the breeze, the way it was reflected in the water. The reflection in the water was kind of beautiful, I remember thinking that, beautiful, even though, if you looked up into the tree, you could see that the real bag ... well, the real bag was all tattered and horrible and was spoiling the look of this lovely tree, wasn't it?

Anyway, there I was, watching this very calm water, it was completely, completely, completely still but with this white ripple dancing away in it, sort of frantic like, like something trying to escape from the still water, but never getting away ... never getting away, when this bloke ... this bloke – Beano, I mean, only I didn't know his name then – anyway, this, this bloke sits down beside me and starts talking to me. I don't know why, I mean, I must have looked like God knows what, I wasn't even washing myself, not even washing myself properly at that stage, not to mind putting on a bit of a face or anything.

And that was that. I never went back, never went back

to Rosie's, did I? I certainly didn't go back to school, that's for sure.

I decided … I decided I was, well, grown up. I'd had to go through all this stuff, I'd had to go through with it all, and I couldn't face going into a place where it was all kids, all kids talking about Ronan Keating and oh, I don't know, Posh Spice and her stupid wedding and her stupid soccer bloke and her stupid baby, kids' stuff, when I, I, I'd been through so much that summer. To me, all that stuff was just stupid, like, it meant nothing any more … it was like sort of, oh, sort of shadow stuff, you know, something that was being, well, being acted out in some other, some silly childish world, but I lived … you see, I lived, I lived in the real world, where people get sick and people die on you and you, well, you lose your parents and your home and everything. When things like that happen to you, you just couldn't be bothered, could you?

And then along came Beano, my hero, I don't think. The mad thing was, the really mad thing was, I was prepared to do anything he said. It was a bit like, well a bit like … being under a sort of a spell, or being hypnotised or something, you know? You know, you see these programmes … these programmes where a hypnotist puts somebody to sleep and then … and then … and then he tells them to take all their clothes off, all their clothes, and run outside and do the Charleston in the street or something really dead stupid and embarrassing, something they wouldn't dream of doing if they weren't hypnotised, and they *do* it, they just do what he tells them, even though it is completely out of character, and everyone is laughing at them. God, it is so embarrassing you sometimes have to turn off the telly, you'd be so mortified for them.

Well, that is the way ... that is the way I was with Beano. I'd never've done the things I done when I was with him, if it hadn't been for him. He had this sort of ... this sort of ... sort of power over me, you know. I mean, let's face it, it was partly because I fancied him something deadly, that was definitely part of it, I suppose I was sort of in love, really, only love is the wrong word ... I know that now, it wasn't love ... because love is supposed to be where the two people, both of them, look out for the other person and want to be with them and want them to be ... you know, happy and all, and they try to make each other happy and they are happy when they are together and lonely when they're apart, isn't that it?

That's my idea of it anyway, but maybe I got all that, maybe I got it all from films or pop songs or something, but I think it's true too. My ma and da, well, they weren't what you'd call romantic ... not romantic, the way they used to roar at each other something dreadful sometimes, but if you said a word ... if you said a *word* against either one of them, the other one would be down your throat, down your throat. They stuck up for each other. I mean, that's what you'd expect, that's what you'd expect, isn't it, if somebody loved you. And that's all really. You can keep all the old romantic stuff ... all the romantic stuff ... as long as somebody loves you and you know that they would always be on your side, no matter what.

Of course, Beano was a great … he was a great actor, he had a great line, a great line in concern. He knew how to worm his way in with you, so that you really thought he thought you were great, so attractive, stunning in fact, and *interesting* – that was the worst part, the way he made you believe he thought you were really interesting – but all he was doing was getting you more and more entangled with him, more and more entangled, so that you'd end up doing whatever it was … whatever it was that he wanted, no matter how disgusting it was. He'd make you believe it wasn't disgusting, wouldn't he? He'd describe whatever you were doing in a totally different way... he'd make you, well, he'd make you see it differently, the way he saw it, the way *he* saw it, as a, well, as a business transaction, something you didn't have to have any feelings about, just something you were doing because it suited you.

'This is what I have to explain to you, Caroline,' he'd say, 'you haven't got the stuff in your head that I have, so for you it's your body that you have to sell, but …' and this is where I want to puke … I want to puke when I think of it, 'remember, you're only lending it to the punters really, you've still got it at the end of the night, it's still your body, and you can sell it again the next night, isn't that great, it's a renewable resource.'

Can you believe, can you believe that shite? He saw me as a *renewable resource*, as if I was a fucking *rain*forest or something. I don't know … I don't know how I let him do that to me, how I let him even *think* of me like that. And he even had *me* thinking of myself like that. That was the dreadful thing. I mean, normally, you know, well … you know right from wrong, you'd know what it's okay to do and what it's not okay to do … you would, I would anyway, the way my ma and da brung me up, but with him around … with him around, you'd lose, you'd lose, you'd lose your sense of that, you know. I hate him for that, for taking that away from me, making me not able to tell the difference between right and wrong, good and bad, okay and not okay.

But all the same, if he walked in … if he walked in that door now, I can't guarantee that I would tell him to eff off with himself. That's what I want, that's what I want to believe I'd do, but I can't be sure, can't be sure I would, because it is just possible, if he put on the right expression, if he said the right words in the right tone of voice, that I would end up going back to him. I know it would be stupid, I know I would end up being sorry, bitter sorry, but I can just see myself doing it, I can just hear myself saying to myself, just one more time, just one more kiss, just one more night.

If I went back to him, though, if I went back … I know I'd never get away again, never, because, you see, I wouldn't have Samantha. It's because of her that I was able, that I was able to get away from him in the first place. But if I went back to him, even for one, even just for one night, that'd be the end of me and Sam, I'm sure of it. She'd give up on me then, for sure, for sure, wouldn't she?

Samantha keeps me going, doesn't she? This place is not very nice really, I mean, it's better than living in a squat, it's cleaner, well, and it's warmer, and it's legal, which sounds stupid, but you get tired of always being afraid someone's going to throw you out, but it's crummy ... it's crummy in its own way, and sometimes it gets terrible crowded with families and kids, doesn't it? We have our own room now, just us two, but sometimes we don't, because, because, because there isn't really enough space so we might have to, we might have to, well, share with another girl, or even a family. And things get nicked on you if you're not careful – not just, not just money, you could understand that, but things ... things like your jeans, you know, things you really can't do without, can you?

Sam makes a big joke out of it all, a big joke. She keeps me going with laughs and seeing, you know, seeing the funny side. She organises little, well, little midnight feasts, even football sometimes, can you imagine, football. No, really ... she organises football games in the middle of, the middle of the night, with the women, up and down the corridors, up and down, when the nunny people are gone to bed, only we have to play real quiet, real quiet, real quiet ... in case we wake them up, but that's half the fun, isn't it, trying to play without making any noise. It sounds, well it sounds daft, but it's great fun. We use one of them soft baby's balls, you know, made of cloth, and we play, we play ... we play in our stocking feet, and we slither up and down and fall and giggle and all the things that worry you during the day –

being pregnant, having nothing, Beano finding us – they all just lift and you forget, you forget … and you just have a good time.

Last night, Sam, she had a date with Curly. I was just getting ready, just getting ready for bed (I need a lot of sleep these days), when, next thing … I heard this shower of little stones on the window. I knew it was Curly, I did, because he often comes, he often comes around in the night-time for Samantha. I do laugh at the pair of them, I do. It's like something out of some old storybook or something, you know like in the song … the song where the woman is spinning or something, and there's a tapping at the window, a tapping, and the young one is off out with the young fella, and the oul' one, the oul' one, she's still spinning away and singing her stupid song, a right eejit she must be.

'There's your man,' says I to Samantha, and I'm unlacing my runners to go to bed, amn't I?

'Ah, come on out with us,' says Samantha.

'And be a gooseberry?' says I. 'Not likely.'

I wasn't … I wasn't really feeling all that great, to tell you the truth. A bit under the weather. Nothing I could … put my finger on. I felt kind of hot and cold, hot and cold. I was wishing I had … well, something, I mean, I'm not hooked, I don't care what they say, I can, I can, I can manage without it, but still, it would've been nice to have a little bit, just to see you through, you know?

'No, you won't be a gooseberry,' says Samantha. 'He's bringing Johnner tonight, so it won't be just the two of us.'

'Ah, you can't be serious,' says I, 'you're not trying to pair me off with *Johnner* are you?'

Samantha, well, she collapsed on the floor laughing, collapsed laughing she did, when I … said that. You would too if you saw Johnner, the size of him, he's only a … only a babby. She was laughing so much, I had to, I had to open the window for Curly, didn't I? 'She'll be out in a minute,' I called out to him, 'just hang on a minute.'

Next thing, Curly's voice comes back: 'Caro, you're to come too, come on now, we want to see you, we want to see how your bump is getting on.'

'Yeah, come on,' says Sam, 'for old times' sake. And of course I'm not trying to pair you off with oul' Johnner, don't be daft, I'm just inviting you to meet our old mates is all. They've been good to us.'

So I said I would, I felt a bit better all of a sudden, and you should've seen me … you should've … you should've seen me wriggling my way out of the window. I mean, I'm not even six months, five and a half maybe, I'm not huge, not huge, but I'm bigger than normal, that's for sure, I really am, amn't I? Curly and Johnner were hiding behind the bushes in the grounds, weren't they? But again they saw me coming, they came to the window and they helped me, they helped me over the windowsill. Sam gave me a push from behind, and between the lot of them, I was like, I was like a cork out of a bottle, and I landed on the gravel and scuffed my hands and knees, but we were all giggling and laughing so much, I hardly even, hardly even noticed it.

We went off down the town and we had two singles

of chips from a chipper – that's all we could, all we could afford. We tried going into … we tried going into an amusement arcade, but we hadn't the money for it, there was no point, no point, was there? So we went back … well, we went back with Curly and Johnner to the squat and we had a few cans and would you believe, Johnner had some *candles*, candles he had, he's a right little, right little pyromaniac, he is, and he lit them, and it was a bit like the night we had the party, wasn't it? We all sat around the candles and we put the sleeping bags over our shoulders and we sat on some beanbags, some beanbags Curly got – we teased him about them, didn't we: 'real homey this place is getting'. And you know, it was better than the party, better than the party really, because everyone was in good form … and no one was stoned … and the best thing was Beano didn't, well, he didn't come crashing in and mess it all up, sure he didn't. It was a lovely night, a really lovely night, and it was lovely to be with your friends, people you can count on. I liked it, I did, didn't I?

Curly and Johnner admired my bump, admired it, and they gave it a little pat and they said it was coming along nicely, and they wanted to know if I could feel it kicking yet.

'Kicking!' says I. 'I'm black and blue with him kicking, he's going to be a kick-boxer, he is.'

Johnner said it might be a girl. Lorraine's baby kicked like mad, he said, and she was a girl, and Samantha, well then, she said, she said maybe she's going to be a can-can dancer, you know, a can-can dancer, like the ones on the cowboy films with the frilly, the frilly bloomers and all the petticoats, that kick their legs up in the air, up in the air. We had a laugh about that, we did, and we tried doing the can-can, doing the can-can around the squat, all of us in a line, with our arms around each other's waists, but we couldn't get the rhythm right, couldn't get it right ... and we kept, we kept ... we kept collapsing in a heap on the beanbags and Samantha said to mind myself I'm in a delicate condition, so then the fellas started fanning me with hankies, putting on funny posh voices, pretending to be butlers or something, and calling me 'your ladyship' all the time.

About two o'clock, though, the candles ... the candles, they gave out, and the place was dark, dark again, and so cold, God, I'd forgotten how cold ... how cold it used to be, so Samantha says we better go home, didn't she? Curly said we could stay if we liked, but Sam said I had to sleep in a proper bed, didn't I? So then Sam made tea to try and warm us all up a bit – she had the torch, they've got batteries ... got batteries for it since. Anyway, after that we left the lads and we headed off back to the hostel.

Again we got out onto the street ... it was lashing, really raining very hard, the gutters were all, all flooded and the streets were covered in water, covered in water, so the road was like a ... like a river, and it was cold, cold rain, and there was a wind too. A horrible night, it was. We got soaked, soaked, going home, but Sam linked me and we put our heads down, and we ran, we just ran a bit of the way, but it was no good ... no good, it was such heavy rain, so heavy that you couldn't keep it out no matter how, no matter … no matter how well you wrapped up or how you ran, so in the end we forgot … we just forgot about, we gave up really, trying to keep dry, and we opened our jackets and we ran, we ran along with our arms spread out, arms spread out, and our mouths open to drink in the rain and we laughed and laughed, didn't we? Then Samantha, she started swinging … swinging out of this lamp-post and she starts singing. 'I'm singing in the rain, I'm singing in the rain, what a glorious feeling, I'm ha-ha-happy again.' That reminded me of … reminded me of my da, didn't it? He used to love them old black-and-white movies. Whenever they came on the telly he used to video them, *Casablanca*, *Singing in the Rain*, all them ones with the fellas in hats and the girls in tight skirts and loads of lipstick.

That was all we knew of the song, so we kept singing just those lines, just those lines, and then we just sang 'I'm ha-ha-happy again,' over and over, and we were kissing the lamp-posts … kissing them … as if they were long-lost friends and skitting laughing, with our hair all hanging down, hanging down, streaming with the rain. We were like people that had fallen into a … into a river or something, we were so wet, weren't we?

When we got home, the place was in darkness, well it would be, wouldn't it, it was nearly three o'clock, and of course it was all locked … all locked up. Normally when Sam gets home at night, I get out of bed and I open the window for her, I do, I open the window to let her in, but this night, we'd just left the window swinging, hadn't we? When we crept around to our room, wasn't somebody after closing it – I suppose it must have been causing a draft somewhere in the house – and we couldn't get in, could we?

We tried throwing gravel at some of the other windows, but it must have been too late – people were in a much deeper sleep than they would be at half-eleven or so when the fellas usually come knocking – and nobody got … nobody got up to us, did they? We tried knocking at the front door then, knocking, because by now we were really chilled right through, like drowned rats we were, but they wouldn't … they just wouldn't answer. They have a policy or something, a policy of not opening the door at night, no matter what. I don't know what they would do, I just don't know, if somebody had called, well, if they had called an ambulance or something, probably tell them to go away and come back in the morning, that this was a disgraceful hour for anyone to have a heart attack!

So we couldn't get in. We had to walk all the way back, all the way back … to the squat then, and it was after four when we got there. We were freezing, freezing we were. The lads gave us towels, didn't they, but no matter how much we rubbed, we couldn't get our hair dry, could we? I went and stood over the gas ring for a bit, sort of waving my hair over it, waving it, but then I singed the ends of it, and the smell was … the smell was awful. Samantha told me I would go on fire if I wasn't careful, so I stopped, it was a bit drier anyway by then. We hung up our clothes and we put on … we put on bits of clothes that the boys had, T-shirts and tracksuits, and we made more tea, to try to warm us up, and Sam rubbed my feet real hard, real hard, to get the circulation going and I rubbed hers, but they were like … they were like dead things they were so cold, I couldn't get any heat into them, could I?

In the end, well, in the end, the two of us got into the one sleeping bag, and it was an awful squash, an awful squash, what with me being larger than life and all, but it was warm, it was warm, even though we had to leave the zip half open. We didn't sleep much, because we couldn't turn without waking the other person up, could we … and when I woke up for good in the morning, I was all stiff … all stiff from the way I was after been lying.

Still, it was a lovely night, even though it didn't end up so great. There was a big clot of bloody stuff in my knickers in the morning. I didn't say anything. I thought it was probably because of all the dancing around in the wet, it puts, well, I suppose it puts a bit of a strain on you, I suppose …

[CUT TO –]
INTERIOR: THE SQUAT – MORNING

Johnner

Hey, it was just like old times here last night, yeah, with the girls being here and all. We had a great night, just us old mates, like, all together, talking and laughing and making jokes. I even had candles again, I did. They were teasing me about them, yeah. They said I should've been an altar boy, I should, they wanted to know was I going to be, like, a priest when I grow up. Curly started singing then, I mean, all this sort of, like, chanty music, you know, not with a proper tune, just about two notes, yeah. He said it was, eh, Latin, but I wouldn't be surprised if he made it up, yeah. Where would he, like, learn Latin? I mean, they don't do it any more, not even for altar boys.

We all sat around on our beanbags, yeah, and everyone's face looked, like, all golden in the candlelight, and Curly was doing his chant, something about *benedictus*, like you'd hear in a monastery, yeah, with the monks all walking along with their hands up their opposite sleeves, the way they do, and, I mean, you'd nearly expect, like, *angels* to appear or something, beautiful it was, even though I knew really that Curly was just taking the piss.

The girls went home at, like, about half-two, but they had to come back because, I mean, they got locked out of that place they're in, it sounds like a boarding school or something, yeah, so they were here in the morning, like. It really reminded me of when we all lived here, yeah, when we were the Kids that Everyone Forgot and we were all having, like, a big adventure together, like camping, like being stranded on a desert island, like living in a candlelit grotto. But that was all before everything started getting all messy, yeah. I mean it was always a bit messy, but then we all had, like, our own messes. Now it's, like, a much bigger mess, and people's messes seem to have got mixed up with each other, like Lorraine and Beano, for example.

I went round to Lorraine's after Caro and Sam left to go home, yeah. I mean, I was kicking around, with nothing much to do, so I thought I'd see how she was getting on like. It wasn't her day for her money, so I didn't expect, like, to bump into Beano again, no way, which is why I thought it would be okay to go this particular day. I walked over, I mean, it's not far, yeah, and I was just coming around by the bike shed, into the yard, where the washing lines are, yeah, and I looked up at Lorraino's flat, I mean, I wanted to see if I could see any sign of life, when what did I see only a *baby* hanging over the balcony, head first.

I didn't stop to think, no way did I, I didn't stop, like, to see who it was, what it was hanging onto, I just headed straight for the stairs, like, and I started leaping up them, yeah, two and three at a time. I must've been yelling and yelling, like, although I don't remember, but I know because my chest is so sore today after it, I must've nearly tearin' my voice box out with the roaring and the racing.

When I got to the balcony, it was Beano, leaning over, and it was Jordan he had, by the ankles like, and he swinging him over the edge. Jordan was screaming and roaring out of him, I mean, real howls of, like, terror, and Beano, he was *laughing*. That was the worst part of it, laughing he was, yeah. Lorraine, she was pulling out of Beano's elbows, yelling at him to put her child down, and he was saying, 'Certainly, missus, I'll put him down,

I'll just let go his ankles here, and down he'll go, wheeeee!'

'Give him to me, Beano, give him to me, please, please, I beg you,' goes Lorraine. 'Give him to me, he didn't do you any harm, he's only two, he's only a baby, please Beano, I'll do anything, just put him… I mean, bring him back in and give him to me.'

And Beano has this, like, fag in his mouth, and he's leaning over and swinging Jordan like a bleedin' yo-yo, and the fag is dropping ash onto the child, and I keep imagining it's going to burn him, only, I mean, it isn't really hot by the time it hits him, it just falls onto his clothes, like, and then breaks up and, like, swirls away in the wind, and Beano is still laughing and swinging the child and *winking* at Lorraine, winking at her, yeah, as if it is all a big joke between them, and that he is doing it to make her laugh.

I didn't know what to do, like. There was no point in going for Beano, no way, because that would only make him drop Jordan. I ran up to him and I started, like, shouting at him the same as Lorraine, but that only made him madder, yeah, so then I leant over the balcony myself, and I made a grab for Jordan.

'Hold onto him, Lorraine,' I yelled, 'hold his arms, immobilise him,' and somehow I managed to get hold of Jordan on the swing towards me.

Lorraine must have gripped something desperate, yeah, because Beano, he wasn't able to break away from her, or anyway, not for the split second that counted – he was at a disadvantage, I mean, because of the way he was bent over the balcony, like, and she was behind him, and I think she must've, like, braced her whole body against him and trapped him between her and the balcony wall, yeah. He gave a roar and he let go of Jordan, but I had him by the arms at this stage, yeah, and then Beano turned on Lorraine and he pushed her onto the floor of the balcony and started kicking her, he did.

I yanked Jordan in, yeah, and I held him in my arms. His face was bright red, the way all the blood had run to his head, and it was covered in snot and in tears, even his hair, and he was screaming so hard I was, like, afraid he wasn't going to be able to breathe, but every now and then he would give this huge breath in, like taking a gulp of water out of a bucket, it was, and then it would come tearing out of him again, the air, covered in, like, snot and blood. His nose had started to bleed, yeah.

I couldn't get Beano off Lorraine, not with the baby in my arms, like, so I went into the flat and I put him down on the settee and I said to Dawn, she was hiding behind the curtains, I mean, I could see her little pink runners sticking out, the ones with the flashing lights, 'Here Dawn, mind Jordan for a minute,' and I ran out again onto the balcony, but Beano had stopped now and he was just lounging back, like, against the balcony wall and sort of grinning, holding his fag by the butt and getting the last few pulls out of it. Lorraine was lying all huddled up at his feet, yeah.

'Well, if it isn't Robin, the Boy Wonder,' says he, grinning at me.

I ignored him and I, like, hunkered down to Lorraine.

'Jordan's okay,' I said to her, 'he's inside, he's okay. Can you stand up?'

She had both hands over her eyes, like, but she peeked out when she saw me, little frightened eyes like a rabbit in a hedge – well, I never actually saw a rabbit in a hedge, but I seen pictures of them in school books – there's always loads of rabbits in school books, I don't know why, since nobody I ever met has ever, like, actually seen one, I don't know why they don't have dogs and cats and mice and rats, the sort of animals we have in the city, but I think they write them books for country kids, all squirrels and rabbits and ladybirds.

Anyway, she got up then, Lorraine did, and she sort of staggered inside, yeah, and, I mean, she sat on the settee, and she picks up Jordan and she's rocking him and rocking him and she's crying and he's crying, and the baby, Debonaire, I can hear her crying in her little basket, but Lorraine, well, I mean, she can't go to her, she has to mind Jordan, so I went over and I picked her up, yeah. I'm kind of used to Jordan's weight, but when I picked up this little thing, she seemed to weigh, like, nearly nothing, just a little scrap, but she made an awful lot of noise for her size. But when I walked up and down with her for a while she stopped roaring, yeah.

Then Dawn comes and sits beside her ma and puts her head on her arm, and she's crying too, and next thing I hear Beano just walking away, off along the balcony and down the stairs. I mean, he causes all this, like, trouble and terrifies everyone, and then off he goes, just walks out. I never even found out what was going on, I mean, why was he tormenting Jordan, what did he want from Lorraine, like, that he did that to a small child? I think he was just doing it to show her that he could. I don't think he's right in the head. He can't be.

But then I saw Lorraine's book on the table. He must've been bringin' it back to her. She must've been payin' him off whatever she owed him, yeah. So he, like, brought it back to her, which is fair enough, and yet he could do that to Jordan. Just showing her how much power he has over her, I suppose, what he can do to her if she doesn't, like, play along with him.

I don't understand anyone that can be like that, I just don't, no way can I understand it.

[CUT TO –]

Samantha

We were jaded in the morning, so we were, after being up so late the night before and getting soaked and all. Curly, fair play to him, he got up early as usual to go to his course. I remember it all very clearly, and that's a fact, I remember the little details, so I do. They say you often do when you've been through a traumatic experience (yeah, okay, I saw a programme about it, what's wrong with that, you have to get your education somewhere). Anyway, I got up early as well, so I did, and I made Curly some tea, because I couldn't sleep anyway with him shuffling around the place getting ready to go. There wasn't any Cornflakes or nothing and I told him he should eat something in the mornings, but then again, he said they get breakfast at the course if they want it.

I brought Caroline a cup of tea as well, so I did. She was all funny looking, and that's a fact, because of getting so wet last night, and because of going to bed without combing her hair, it was all sticking out, so it was. I told her she looked as if she slept in herself. She said she did.

She didn't get it. I tried to explain, you know how you say to someone they look as if they slept in their clothes, well, she looked as if she slept in her*self*. She still didn't get it, so I gave up.

I told her to try to get some more sleep, so I did, and she lay down again for a bit after she finished her tea, but she couldn't, so she got up after a while and she said she wanted to go home, she said she might sleep a bit if she could get into her own bed. She wasn't feeling all that great, she said. So anyway, Johnner lent us a comb and some soap, and we tidied ourselves up a bit, so we did, and we started off home.

The streets were dead busy, so they were, because it was the morning time, everyone mad to get to work, I suppose. You'd think they wouldn't want to, you'd think they'd be dragging their feet, wouldn't you? The way I did when I was going to school, wishing I wasn't going to get there, but they must get into trouble if they're late, because they were all in a mad rush, fair play to them. It was like Henry Street during the sales, so it was, but we kept going, we did, and we were just near the bridge when suddenly Caroline gave a shout:

'Jaysus, Samantha, I'm soaked.'

She sat down in the middle of the street, so she did, and she was pulling her knees up to her chest, and sort of moaning, so she was.

'What's wrong, Caro?' I asked. She said she wasn't feeling too good. I thought maybe she was sweating or something, with a fever you know, when she said she was soaked. She didn't answer, so she didn't, she just kept rocking back and forward on the street and saying, 'I'm soaked, I've wet myself.'

Well, pregnant women do sometimes, you know, they can't control themselves always, I knew someone once where I lived before, so I did, one of the workers, she was pregnant, and she told me all about it. At the time, I didn't really want to know the details, but I'm glad now, so I am.

So anyway, I sat down beside Caroline and I said, 'It's okay, Caro, it doesn't matter, sure it's only Curly's old tracksuit you're wearing, come on and we'll get home and you can have a wash and get changed.'

I stood up then and I put out my hand to her and she grabbed it, so she did, and she stood up too, but as soon as she did, I could see this huge wet place on her tracksuit. It wasn't just a little bit of pee, I could see that, and it was spreading and spreading, so it was.

'Oh Jesus!' I yelled. I shouldn't have yelled, I'm sure I frightened her, but I got a fright myself, so I did. 'Oh Caro, Jesus.'

She looked down at herself then, and she watched the wet spreading, and she said, 'Is it blood?'

'No,' I said, 'it's not blood.'

'That's okay, so,' says she, 'isn't it?'

I didn't say anything.

Then it struck her. 'If it's not blood, what is it, Sam?' she asked in this really small voice.

'I think it's your waters,' I said.

'What's that?' she asked, looking at me real puzzled, her eyes were open extra wide, so they were, wide enough for the terror to shine out.

'It's something pregnant women have,' I said. 'Look, I think we better get you to the hospital.'

She didn't want to go, she started shaking, she had her hand to her mouth and she shook, so she did, but she said, the words coming out between her fingers, 'As long as it's not blood, that's all right, isn't it Samantha, I don't need to go to the hospital. I can just go home and go to bed for a while, can't I?'

She hates hospitals. I had a terrible job persuading her, so I had. I kept looking around to see if anyone could help, I thought I might be able to get someone to ring for an ambulance, but even though there were millions of people, they were all just flying along, so they were, nobody was looking at us, I couldn't catch anyone's eye.

'Come on, Caro,' says I, 'it's better to see the doctor, just to make sure you're okay. Anyway, we need to sit down. You can't walk all the way home from here, but we'll make it to the Rotunda if we take it easy.'

I put my arm around her waist, so I did, and I put her arm around my shoulders, and we sort of staggered back up O'Connell Street, so we did. It took us forever, it did, and we got a few funny looks, I think people thought she was drunk – imagine, a pregnant girl drunk at half-nine in the morning in the middle of O'Connell Street – but we made it anyway.

They knew as soon as they saw her, and that's a fact. They whisked her away before I could explain anything. They wouldn't let me come with her, so they wouldn't. They put her on this big trolley thing and they were shouting all these questions at her, I could hear them as they went off down the corridor, they were asking her what religion she was, God, I expected the trolley and the shouting, because I used to watch a lot of ER, but what religion is she! They never ask that in ER, so they don't.

It was only later it struck me they should know her religion already, if they really need to know. They must have her records somewhere. This is where she comes to the clinic – or where she says she's been coming. The little wagon, she mustn't have been going to the clinic at all. She *said* she was, but I know she hates hospitals. She must've mitched off, she's a holy terror, she is, you'd want eyes in the back of your head.

I should've been goin' with her, I knew I should, I knew she hated going. It's all my fault, so it is. It's always someone's fault, and this time it's mine, so it is.

I sat there for a long time, and nothing happened and then I went out for a smoke, so I did. I met a few of the fathers, and they were laughing at me, teasing me, asking me was it mine or what, was I the father, like? Jaysus, I nearly kicked them in the balls, so I did. The only reason I didn't was that I didn't want to get arrested, because then I wouldn't be any use to poor Caroline …

[CUT TO –]

INTERIOR: HOSPITAL ROOM – DAYTIME

Caroline is lying in bed, talking to the ceiling.

Caroline

I called him … I called him James. They said, well, they said you have to give the baby a name. I looked at him when they said that. He was lying here, just right here beside me, in a little cot, just beside my bed, and he was … he was all wrapped up in a tiny little, tiny little white blanket. I don't know why they left him there, I couldn't do anything for him, could I?

He didn't look like a baby, did he? Not a proper baby. He looked like, well, he looked like a little bird, little birdy chest, little birdy arms, little tiny birdy legs and feet, tiny little willy like a curl. His head, his head was too big for his little birdy body, it looked like it might fall off if you didn't hold it. He looked like … he looked like you could break him if you applied any pressure, like breaking the wishbone.

I used to pull … I used to pull … the wishbone with my ma when I was small, didn't I? She used to put it on the heater, on the heater, to let it dry out, you know, because … because … because I couldn't get a grip on it when it was all, all slithery, and when it was dry we used to … we used to hook our little fingers around it and we used to ... to wish with our eyes closed, didn't we? And then we pulled, and my ma used to say it didn't matter, it didn't really matter who got the biggest piece, that as long as we both wished hard enough, one of the wishes, one of them would come true, wouldn't it?

I used to wish for a little sister, most of the time. That was okay, it was okay, because you weren't supposed to tell the wish, sure you weren't? I wouldn't want her to know ... my ma, I wouldn't want her to know that that's what I was wishing for. I used to add on a PS that a little brother would do. Sometimes, sometimes, sometimes I wondered if that sort of spoilt it, spoilt the wish, tacking a bit on, and maybe that's why it didn't work out, ever, maybe that's why.

When I was older, my ma, she explained it, she explained it all to me. After she was cured of the cancer, well, cured the first time, the doctor, he told her it would be safer not to get pregnant again, that it might, well, that it might reactivate it, so that's why she didn't have any more kids, and that's why my wish never came true.

Oh well, oh well, that's the end of my family now, the end of them all, I thought to myself, looking at the little birdy thing they told me was my baby. It's hard to believe. It's real hard to believe. He'd fit in ... he'd fit in the palm of your hand, wouldn't he? I mean, you couldn't hold him in your arms, he'd smother, no that doesn't make any sense, no sense, but I mean he'd disappear, he'd be lost, wouldn't he?

You know, I had this horrible thought, really horrible.

I don't know if I thought it all by myself, or if somebody said it or what, at some stage when I was out of it, you know? The thought was, God, I can hardly say it, it was: maybe, well, maybe this is all for the best.

That's the sort of thing people said when my ma died, and when my da died, 'All for the best,' they said, all for the best ... out of their misery and all that. That's where I got this idea that maybe people would think that about James, too. The poor little bird, he never had a chance, had he? Never got a go, never got a go at life at all, but maybe people would just say it was all for the best, that he's better off, you know, that I wouldn't be any good ... no good as a ma, too young, too silly, too unsettled, too poor. And he hasn't got a da at all, no da, or not one that counts, anyway, so maybe he's better off wherever he is, with God, I suppose, in Heaven.

Even, some people might say, that it's a sort of, well, some sort of judgement on me. That is ... that really is a horrible idea, isn't it? It wouldn't be fair on him, would it, he done nothing on nobody, and look at him now, poor little scrap. It breaks my heart, doesn't it?

It breaks my fuckin' heart.

He looks like my da, even with his face all tiny ... all tiny and screwed up, he has that little dimple just at the side of his mouth. Isn't it amazing how that sort of thing gets passed on, even in ... even ... even in ... a little bit of a thing, a nothing nearly, like him? But it's a little bit of my da all the same, and there it is, in that little cot there, in that little cot ... even though it's nearly a year since, since my da died, isn't it? It's funny to have ... to have a little bit of him back like that, only it's not really back, it's only on loan, just for a day or two.

God, it's all awful, awful, I just want to die and be done with it.

I want my baby, oh, I *want* my baby.

I asked them where Samantha was. They said, who's Samantha? Is she my next-of-kin, they wanted to know, my next-of-kin. I said what's next-of-kin, and they said, they said your nearest relation, and I said, 'He is, James, the baby, he's my next-of-kin.' So then they wanted to know … they wanted to know where my ma and da were, and I just looked at them and shook, shook my head. They said, 'Do they not know, is that the problem, did you not tell them you were pregnant?' and I shook my head again, and she wrote something, she wrote something down on a clipboard, the nurse did.

She went away then, that nurse, and I lay there for a while, didn't I, looking at a crack on the ceiling. I was in a room of my own, but the door was open, and I could hear … I could hear all these sounds, people racing up and down corridors, up and down, babies, babies, babies crying, everywhere babies crying, but they sounded far away, even though … even though I knew they were just close by. I wondered what it would be like … what it would be like to hear your baby crying, would you be annoyed or would you be glad?

I think you'd be glad really, wouldn't you? Yeah, you'd have to be, I think, you would be glad.

Then this man … this man came to see me. He told me he was a priest. He wasn't wearing proper priest's clothes, was he? He had on a cardigan, a cardigan with a zip. He sat down … he sat down beside my bed and he put his hand on top of the back of my hand, but I slid my hand out from under his and I put it under the blankets, didn't I?

I kept looking … just kept looking at the ceiling. I followed the crack right into the corner, and I noticed that it went down the wall a good eighteen inches, didn't it? This building is going to fall down, going to fall down, I thought to myself, it has structural problems, it has, but I didn't … I didn't really care, really I didn't. Then it would all be over … all over … and I wouldn't have to worry any more. I smiled, I actually smiled when I thought that thought. It made me feel light in the head, didn't it?

Then the priest started asking me if there was anyone, anyone, anyone I wanted to see, so I said Samantha, didn't I? And he said who's Samantha? And I said she was my friend, my friend, well, my friend that came in with me, so he said he would talk to the nurses and ask them to find her, and I said 'Thank you, Father.' I don't know … I don't know how I remembered to call him father, when he was wearing the cardigan. It's funny how your mind can be very clear sometimes when you'd expect it to be fuzzy, can't it?

Then he said … he said he was going to say a prayer with me. I thought, well, I thought he would go and look for Samantha first, but he wanted … he wanted to say this prayer. I looked at him. He said did I mind, and I didn't say anything. It seemed, well, it seemed a pointless sort of thing to me, when he could be out looking for Sam for me, but I didn't care what he said, really, so he starts on the … Hail Mary.

When he gets to 'And blessed is the fruit of thy womb,' I started to scream, I started to scream, didn't I? It was that word, 'womb', it just … well, it just set me off, didn't it? I screamed and screamed and screamed and screamed. I wasn't … I wasn't crying. I wasn't lashing about, even, was I, I was just lying there on my back … with the sheet, the sheet pulled up to my chin and my hands under the blankets, screaming at, screaming at the ceiling.

I don't know … I don't know why I screamed. I think I just wanted him to go away … go away and leave me alone. He jumped up and he ran out, ran out, and I smiled to myself, didn't I?

Then I went on, well, I just went on screaming. I wanted to see what would … what would happen next, didn't I, how long it would take for someone to come and try to stop me.

Another nurse … another nurse came running in then, not the one, not the one with the clipboard, and she comes over to the bed and she slaps me twice on the face, once on each cheek. Not in a horrible way, not angry, just business-like, like it's a treatment or something, so I stopped screaming, didn't I?

I could feel the sting … I could feel it, on my cheeks, where she'd hit me, and I imagined … I imagined there would be two big red handprints on my face, and that made me smile, and soon the smile, well, the smile turned into a little rumbling laugh, and I couldn't keep the laugh in, I just couldn't … and it started pouring out of me, pouring out, pouring out of the corners of my mouth and dribbling down onto my pillow and I could feel my whole body shaking with the laugh, and in the end I gave up trying to keep it in and I opened my mouth and let it come out and I laughed and laughed and laughed, I had to turn onto my side because I was choking with the laughing, wasn't I, and all the time the nurse just stood there watching me, just … just stood there, and when the laugh began to fade away, she stroked my hair, stroked my hair she did, and she says, real ordinary, as if nothing had happened, 'Okay, Caroline?'

I thought … well, I thought that was dead nice. She didn't even know me, she never saw me in her life before, but she knew to stroke my hair, didn't she? I thought she'd give out to me … give out to me for laughing. I nodded, and she said, 'I'll be back in a minute.'

She went off and in a minute she was back with a little paper cup of water, and one of them long tablets, and she said to take it, it was Valium. I said okay, so I took it, didn't I, and then I asked her to find Samantha for me, and she didn't ask who Samantha was, she didn't ask stupid questions, she didn't, she just asked the first sensible question I'd heard since I got here, she said where was she? And I said she'd brought me in and she was probably downstairs still. I knew she wouldn't go away.

She asked me what was Samantha's other name, and I said, I think I was getting a bit woozy at this stage from the Valium, I said, 'Sam, that's her other name. Her real name is Samantha, but her other name is Sam.' She said all right, she'd find her, and she went off then, off she went, and she closed the door, didn't she, and so then there was just me and James and the silence.

[HOLD]

Complete silence, then CUT TO –

INTERIOR: THE SQUAT – EVENING

Curly

I was making a sandwich for the tea, for me and Johnner, right, just the two of us. We done this stuff on nutrition, see, on my course, and they said a sandwich was as good as a meal, right, if you put the right stuff into it, stands to reason, I reckon. The right stuff is, I dunno, meat or fish, like tuna or sardines or something, or you could use cheese instead, only I hate cheese, and you have to have something vegetably like, you know, grated carrots or chopped up lettuce, plus the bread is supposed to be brown, but Johnner, well he only eats white bread so that's what we had. The way I see it, white bread is better than no sandwich, and it's much better than them ould crisps he's forever eating, the pasty-faced little individual.

The woman said a sambo like that has the main things you need, see, stands to reason, carbo-something to fill you up and give you energy, right, that's the bread, protein, that's the meat and that's just good for you, I can't remember why, right, and the vegetably stuff is for, let me see, the vitamins and things, I think, and I can't remember what they're for either, but I know you have to have them or you get scampy, right, and you die. That's what she said anyway, she said sailors used to die of scampy because they lived on biscuits. Imagine dying from eating biscuits. It makes you think, doesn't it.

She said if we had a good sandwich with a glass of milk or orange juice, you could live on it and you'd be fine. I said you could live on burgers and chips, that's the way I look at it, and she said it would cost more, and anyway you wouldn't be getting the right balance of foods, so I said I'd give it a go, though I have to say I think food should ideally be hot, that's the way I look at it, anyway.

Of course, I didn't have anything to grate carrots with, that's a bit much, I thought to myself, but anyway, I was improvising with slices of apple instead (my teacher, Linda, says I'm very resourceful, right), I was using the apple because, the way I look at it, fruit is nearly the same as vegetables, I reckon, they all grow anyway, right, stands to reason, and so there I was making ham and apple sandwiches and Johnner was breaking his sides laughing at me slicing up the apple, he said I was getting more and more like Samantha. I said there was nothing wrong with that, that Samantha has the right idea about lots of things, see. I told him it was time he started eating healthy, right. I said he sounded as if he was going to cough up his lungs right onto the floor some day, and he better start getting the right food into him, at least.

He was having none of it, Johnner wasn't. 'Have you no crisps?' he says, 'only I like crisp sandwiches,' and I said to him to get up the yard with his crisp sandwiches, that I'd as soon brain him with a bag of crisps, right, as soon brain him as put them in a sandwich for him, so there we are, laughing and joking, right, and Johnner is saying it's too healthy for him altogether this food and that he needs to have his grease quotient every day. Grease quotient! Where does he get expressions like that out of? I dunno, he'd surprise you sometimes, young Johnner, it's hard to know what he's going to come out with next. So I said I wouldn't make him drink orange juice with it, in case he got healthy too fast and his system couldn't cope, so we had a can of Coke instead.

It was very nice, I have to say, a bit unusual, but very tasty, and Johnner took it all back, he did, what he said about the crisps, and he even asked me if I'd make him another one. I was just getting it for him, right, when next thing Samantha arrives in, looking all frazzled and upset like, and she's still wearing an old pair of jeans I gave her this morning when her clothes were wet from the rain last night, so she mustn't have been home at all, and now it's six o'clock in the evening, right, and as soon as she sees the food, she says, 'Oh God, Curly, I didn't have a bite to eat all day, make me a sandwich for the love of God.'

So I did, and I gave it to her, right, and in between mouthfuls she's telling us this terrible story about Caroline. I couldn't follow it all, she started having the baby on the street, I think, it was all women's stuff. I don't listen to them when they start on that stuff about their bodies, because it makes me faint, I don't know how they put up with it all, every month, and then having babies as well, and leaking and everything, God, it's horrendious really, when you think about it, so I don't think about it much if I can help it, that's the best thing, is the way I look at it.

'But she's not even six months,' I said – I know that much about women, I'm not that bad, it takes nine months to have a baby – 'that's what she said last night, less than six months.'

'Yeah,' says Samantha, real quiet like, 'that's the problem, isn't it.'

'Oh well,' I said, trying to cheer her up, like, 'at least she's too far gone to *lose* it.' I thought you could only lose a baby very early on, you know, before people even knew you were pregnant – shows what I know, doesn't it?

She gave me this funny look, and then she bit into her sandwich real hard, and as she did that, she gave this yelp, see. I thought she was after bitin' her tongue, I did, and I put my hand under her chin and I said 'Here, spit it out, Sam, spit it out!' I was afraid she was going to choke she was yelling so hard, but she did as I said and she spat it out into my hand, right, half mushed up and chewed, and I threw it in a plastic bag we have for a bin, see.

Well, anyway, I was so busy cleaning up my hand and everything, right, that I didn't realise Sam wasn't cursing just because she'd hurt herself. It began to dawn on me that she was crying too hard for somebody who'd only bit their tongue.

'Here, Sam,' I said then, and I put my arms around her, right, and she was sobbing fit to break your heart, and over the top of her head, I could see Johnner was white as a sheet, just staring at the floor, which is not like him at all, he's usually bouncing around the place, cracking jokes, sometimes he can be really annoying the way he keeps bobbing around, but he was just sitting very still, only his jaws moving – he went on munching his sandwich, real sort of dogged like, as if he needed something to concentrate on that wasn't Sam and Caroline, that's the way I see it, anyway.

'What's wrong, Sam, love, what is it?' I was asking. 'Is it Caro, is she not all right?'

But she couldn't answer, she was crying too hard. Her hair was all over her face, right, and there was little flecks of half-chewed bread stuck on her face and even caught in her hair, and she was making these retching sounds, see, as if she couldn't get in enough air between her sobs.

So anyway, I just held her for a long time, and I rocked her, the way you do with a child, and she was clutching onto me, real hard, as if she was afraid she was going to lose me or something. Then after a while she starts to slow down, and she's snatching longer breaths, and then after a little while she stopped crying altogether.

So then, I was combing her hair back off of her face with my fingers, tucking it in behind her ears for her and wiping the little bits of sandwich off, when next thing she starts off again, with a fresh wail, and she was off on another crying fit. Three or four times that happened, crying and crying and then calming down, and taking off again after a minute, but each time she set off again, it wasn't as bad as the time before, see, it was sort of softer, you know? And anyway, by the end there were just ordinary tears, right, no more huge gasping sobs any more, and after about ten minutes she calmed down enough to have a few sips of Coke. She wouldn't eat any more, she said she couldn't, even though she just said she was starving. I dunno, doesn't make sense, but that's women for you.

Johnner was finished eating by now and he was tidying up, putting the sliced pan away in its wrapper and throwing stuff in the bin – Johnner swears he saw a rat here one day, so we have to be very careful about food, that's the way I look at it. He was moving around the place real slow and careful, as if Samantha was a child that was asleep that he didn't want to wake up, see.

I still didn't know what was going on. I thought Caroline must have got some terrible disease, right, that women get from having babies or something, purple fever I think they call it, I remember hearing my ma talking about somebody she knew that died of it, so I thought that must be it, stands to reason that'd be what was wrong.

I wondered if Caroline was dead. I couldn't imagine that. She was here this morning, snoring in a sleeping bag when I left, I couldn't believe she could be lying dead in some hospital by teatime. It seemed like something that would happen in India or somewhere, not here, see. But anyway, it wasn't Caroline, it was the baby, Sam said.

[CUT TO -]

Johnner

We all went to the funeral, eh, me and Curly and Sam. Lorraine wanted to come too, terrible cut up about Caro's baby, she was, I think it's because of Debonaire, being so young and all, makes her, like, feel it worse. But she won't leave the kids with anyone these days, not after what Beano done to Jordan, and she didn't want bringing them all. But she got this lovely card for Caroline, not, like, a dead card, a nice one with all flowers on it, and she wrote 'Thinking of you, Caroline' on it and all these kisses at the bottom, and she gave it to me to give to Caro, like, and Caro put it on the little coffin.

There was a woman there as well as us, yeah, and she had two kids with her, a bit younger than me, a boy and a girl, like, and they were fidgeting and looking embarrassed, I don't know who they were, and there was two nurses as well, one of them had her arm around Caroline, like.

I didn't know they done funerals for babies that die when they're born before their time, I thought that was, like, a miscarriage, but anyway, they do, and Sam said Caro would like us all there, yeah. I wondered if we should tell Beano. Well, I mean, it's his baby too (I think), but Samantha nearly crucified me when I said that, she asked me did I want Caroline to have a nervous breakdown or wha'. I said of course I didn't, I was only, like, wondering.

We didn't see it, it was all in its little, you know, eh, coffin, like a wedding cake it was, when we got there, but Sam seen it. She gave Caroline this little vest she'd got for the baby and Caro put it on and they were laughing, the two of them, the way it was miles too big. I thought that was a bit off, really, that they were, like, laughing about it, it doesn't seem right to be laughing about a thing like that, yeah, but that's what Sam said anyway, that they were laughing about it. She said it looked like a little scarecrow, but anyway, Caro said she wanted him to wear the little vest, even though it didn't fit, like, because that was Samantha's present to him, and Samantha was his godmother.

I said was he baptised, and Samantha said of course he was, what did I think, was Caro a heathen or something, I said I didn't know, I never heard of her going to mass or nothing, and I asked was Sam there at the baptism, and Sam said no, but she was its godmother anyway, because that was what Caro wanted, and would I, like, stop asking questions. So I did.

It wasn't like a real funeral, just a few prayers in this chapel place, yeah, and there was this priest, he had this funny zipped-up cardigan on under, you know, that frilly blouse thing they wear when they're doing the masses and things, I could see it peeping out over the lace, and he said would somebody read, and he looked around and he pointed at *me*.

I nearly collapsed, I did. I can read, don't get me wrong, I can, but I don't like doing it when other people can hear me, and I do have to put my finger, like, under the words or I lose my place and people laugh at me sometimes. But anyway, he kept pointing at me, this priest did, so I went up, and there was this huge book, with nice big writing in it, I wish all books had writing like that, I mean, it would be much easier to read if they had, yeah. It had this bit in it, 'suffer the little children'. I thought that was, like, an awful thing to say to a dead baby, I mean really sort of rubbing it in, but nobody else said anything, like, so I read on, it was only a few lines, yeah, and when I was finished, I could hear Caroline crying, and Samantha was holding her head and patting her hair and she was whispering to her, but when I went back to my seat, Curly gave me, like, a slap on the back and he said I done great. I bet he was glad it wasn't him, he's worse than me, like, at the reading, even though he's older.

I thought it was the saddest thing anyone ever asked me to do, yeah, to read a story for a baby that was dead, but I done it when I was asked, and I was glad, and afterwards, Caroline kissed me. A girl never kissed me before. It was very nice, sort of fluttery and warm at the same time, and it made me feel all woo-y inside.

I liked it. But I'd have preferrin' if it wasn't at a funeral, all the same.

[Music and FADE OUT]

PART 5

a pig in shit

FADE IN

INTERIOR: A CAFÉ – DAYTIME

Samantha and Curly are at a table, drinking tea, talking in whispers, giggling quietly. Then Samantha looks up and speaks TO CAMERA.

Samantha

It's funny how things work out, and that's a fact. I mean, one minute, there we are, me and Caro, living in the hostel place, so we are, larking about kissing lamp-posts, and three days later Caro's gone off back to live with her auntie and her cousins, and it's all over, so it is, me and Caro being together and minding the baby and everything and maybe getting a flat together, all over and done with, those plans, buried out in Glasnevin cemetery with all the Baby Angels – that's what they call them, babies like James, something like that anyway.

It was me told the nice nurse, Jenny her name is, about Caro's auntie Rosie, so it was. I told her she must live out

Tallaght way, so she must, Rosie, because I remembered that Caro was catching a 49 to go and see her the day I met her. I can't imagine how Jenny worked it out, she must be dead clever, so she must, but anyway, she tracked her down and she told her about Caroline, and so she came with two of her kids – they must be Caro's cousins, I suppose – anyway, they all came to the funeral we had for James, and afterwards we all went back to her house and we had soup out of a huge big pot that Rosie made, she's a great cook, fair play to her, it was lovely, so it was, and we had cake too, and everyone was nice to Caroline and she was great, she didn't even cry once the chapel bit was over, she was sort of serene, I suppose you would call it. I suppose she's used to funerals, God help her.

So anyway, Caro is going to stay with her auntie for a while, so she is, because her auntie says she needs looking after, but she said to me I done a great job with Caro, I was a real friend. I am too. I mean, I'm not boasting now, or nothing, but I know I done my best for her, and even though I didn't make her go to her clinics and all, still, I done what I could, so I did. I'm kind of glad the auntie is minding her now, because I think she needs proper people to look after her now, grown-ups.

Anyway, Rosie says that I can come out to see her any time and I can stay the night if I don't mind sharing with Caroline, as if I would.

I wish I had a ma like her, so I do. Even an auntie would do. I bet she makes shepherd's pie on Mondays and makes them kids do all their home ekker before she lets them watch the telly. That's the sort of her, so it is.

But anyway, the good news is – don't laugh, now – me and Curly is getting engaged. Imagine!

> [Samantha turns to Curly and kisses him shyly. He kisses her back, and then, turning to speak TO CAMERA, he takes up the story.]

Curly

I dunno, I asked her on the way home on the bus from Rosie's house, after the funeral for the baby. She nearly fell off the seat, she was totally gobsmacked. She told me not to be daft, we were too young to get married.

I was ready for that one, I have to say, I *knew* she'd say that, so I said look at Caroline, she's too young for that to happen to her, but it did, see, there's no such thing as too young, really. She looked at me for a long time after I said that, and you know I could tell she was thinking that was a very brainy thing for stupid old Curly to say …

> [sound of Samantha laughing softly in the background.]

… but I'd been thinking about it for a long time, right. I worked it out that when you're like us, see, and you've got nothing, well then you've only got each other, and then I thought if we've got each other, that's better than nearly anything else, you know, better than a proper place or a job or money or anything, right, stands to reason, the way I see it, because lots of people have all them things, right, but they haven't got each other, so really we're better off.

I know, I know, I know it sounds sappy, but it's true when you think about it. Just because something sounds sappy doesn't mean it's not true.

I tried to explain all this to Samantha, but of course Samantha being Samantha and not a romantic bone in her body, she said that was a load of horseshit, right, that there was loads of people who thought love was enough and they soon learned that it wasn't when they didn't have enough money, right, and kids started coming along and love flew out the window soon enough.

God, it was hard work, it was, I can tell you.

So then I said, well, look at it this way, there's old Caro now, and she's had a terrible rough time, right, and Beano was all wrong for her anyway, and she had all that stuff happening to her with her ma and da as well, but that *if* Beano *had* been right for her, and if he'd stood by her and loved her enough, well, he couldn't have made it all all right, but it would have *helped*, right, that's the way I see it.

Well, she had to agree with that, you can't deny that, can you, but then she started going on about what a wanker Beano is, which is true, but I wasn't going to let this turn into a conversation about Beano, so I said look here, Sam, this is about you and me, see, and whether we are right for each other, and she said of course we were, but there was no need to get *married*, that was going a bit far, see.

Well, I said, no, it wasn't, that there's all these people and they're together for a while and then they have a baby, right, and maybe they're still together after that, okay, and then maybe they have another baby, and then maybe they say, hey, we should really get married, we're beginning to look like a family, see, and so maybe they get married then – or of course, maybe they don't.

And she said, Sam, I mean, she said, 'What's that got to do with the price of eggs?'

Well, I didn't know what she was going on about, I don't like eggs, me. So I ignored that question and I said what I *meant* was, that that was doing it all arseways, that's the way I look at it, that people were having babies first, right, and then getting married, and next thing they'd be getting engaged and then after about six months they might get introduced.

She laughed at that, but she still said, she didn't see what it had to do with the price of eggs. I don't know what she keeps going on about eggs for, I really don't see where eggs come into it, see, but I stuck to my guns and I said, look, having babies is very hard, and she said too right it was, you'd want to hear the screams coming from the labour ward in the Rotunda, and I said I didn't mean that, that was only the *start* of it, see.

So then I said that if people are going to have babies, well then, they need help, you can't do it by yourself, it's not fair on women to have to do it all by themselves, that they should have someone to help them, that that's how it's supposed to be, that's why men and women are different, and that's why men can't have babies, stands to reason.

'Wow!' she said, and she mopped her brow, I mean

she really did, she took out a tissue and she gave her forehead a good wipe. Then she picked up my hand and she starts feeling my pulse.

'Look,' I said, 'maybe I'm saying this all wrong …'

'Em, yes, maybe you are,' says Samantha, all reasonable-like. 'Maybe, like, you have this really, really, really, very, *very* old-fashioned idea about women, could that be it? Maybe you think we're just for having babies, Curly? Well, there's more to it …'

Well, I had to stop her before she went off into a big women's lib thing. 'No,' I said, and I'm starting to get a bit sort of edgy, like, afraid the conversation is going off all in the wrong direction. 'No, I don't think that, right, but I do know that babies come into it, see, and there's no point in pretending they don't because if you do, you end up with a situation like Beano and Caro.'

Well, there I had her, hadn't I? That was certainly true. I had it all worked out, I had, see, I thought about it all.

'Right,' she says, 'okay, keep going. What's the next bit of this argument?'

'Well,' I said, 'that's all really. There has to be one that doesn't have the babies but whose job is to do the helping, and that's the fella, right?'

She didn't know what to make of that one, right, I could see I had her cornered now. She's not as clever as she thinks she is, but I don't blame her, because it took me a very long time to work all this out, and I was trying to explain it all to her in five minutes on a number 49 bus.

Anyway, I said, 'Look Sam, what it comes down to is this, I'd like us to be together, right, and, well, maybe later, when we're more settled, to have kids, but I'd like us to do it together and I'd like us to be together properly, like forever, if we can manage that – I'm not saying we can, now, but that's what I'd like – because that's the *right* way to do it, and so, will you marry me?'

And she said, 'God, Curly, you're a right Romeo, you are, that's a funny reason to want to get married.'

Well that was a stupid answer, wasn't it, because really it's the *only* reason to get married, that's the way I look at it, but I didn't want to annoy her, so I didn't argue any more, I just kept looking at her, right, looking right into her eyes and willing her to say yes.

She turned away then and she looked out the window and she said, 'Well, em …'

'Yes?' I said.

'Well, you're supposed to be the romantic one,' she said then. 'So what happened to champagne and roses and a ring?'

'I couldn't afford *all* them things,' I said, and then I really surprised her, right, because I put my hand in my pocket and I produced the ring. She went white. She really did. She couldn't believe it. She clapped her hand over her mouth and she stared at it.

'It's not real,' I said, 'the diamond's not real, it's only glass, it's a cheap one, but I paid for it, I didn't knock it off, and it's what I could afford, so until I can get you a better one, will it do?'

I thought she was going to give me another lecture about women's lib and all this stuff and how she wouldn't wear any man's ring, not if it was made of

22-carat diamonds, but guess what she did? She burst into tears.

But then real suddenly she stopped crying and she said, 'Curly Daly, I love you, and I never want another ring as long as I live,' and next thing there was this cheer, see, all the people on the bus were listening in, I nearly died I was that mortified, and Johnner was cheering too, he was on the seat behind us, I'd forgotten he was there, and he starts thumping me on the back and saying, 'Good on ya, Curly, go on, you good thing you!'

So anyway, that's the story, but of course, Samantha is dead sensible, right, so she said she wasn't coming back to live in the squat, that she was going to stay in the hostel, and she's going to do a child-care course, see. There's a change – Sam swore she'd never sit in a classroom again, but I suppose as you go through life, you have to change your mind about things, haven't you, or you'd never grow and develop at all, you'd be stuck the way you always were, that's the way I look at it. Anyway, she said she was talking to one of the people that runs that place where she lives and they were going to fix her up with a course, because she wants to mind babies and children, right, she realised that, she said, when Caro was pregnant, and then when she gets settled and maybe gets a job, and if I can get a job or even an apprenticeship off my Youthreach, then we can *maybe* get a place together, and maybe then we can *think* about getting married, if we still think we want to, but we don't have to unless we're sure, see.

'So are we engaged, then?' I asked her, because this all

sounded a bit maybe-ish to me. It's hard to know with Samantha sometimes.

'Maybe,' she said.

'Ah, Sam, come on!' I said.

'Well, all right,' she said. 'We can say we're *getting* engaged, will that do?'

I didn't push it, right. I think that's as far as Sam is going to go, and that'll do me now, for the moment.

Anyway, I asked Linda did she think I might be able to train as a chef, that I liked the nutrition stuff we done, and I'd like to learn cooking properly, and she said she'd do her best to find out about it for me, so that's my next plan of action.

We're talking about all this stuff, these plans, on the bus on the way back into town, and suddenly Sam turns round to Johnner, right, and she says, 'And as for you, young fella-me-lad, you are going back to school. I'll give you till September, you can have the summer off, but on the first of September you are getting that school-bag together and you're going to school, you hear? I'm not having you turning into a waster, so I'm not, you might end up like Beano. And if I see so much as a single aerosol, even the whiff of it, you'll be in deep shit with me, you hear me now?'

Johnner gave her a puck on the shoulder, but he didn't say no, he never argued with her. Maybe he'll do it. He thinks a lot of Sam, he does.

So that's me and Sam anyway. Great, isn't it? I think so anyway, I'm as happy as a pig in shit, I am.

Music: 'The Sweetest Thing' by U2 and FADE OUT.

Also for Older Readers
Books for age 15+

ALLISON:
A STORY OF FIRST LOVE
Tatiana Strelkoff

When Karen meets Allison, her world is turned upside down. What are these feelings she has towards this girl? Why do they make her both uncomfortable and excited? And, most importantly, how will her parents and brother react? Should she turn her back on her feelings?

Paperback £5.99

WHEN LOVE COMES TO TOWN
Tom Lennon

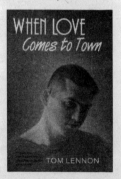

Meet Neil Byrne – try-scorer on the rugby field, prize-winning student, one of the in-crowd at the disco, regular guy, gay.

Presenting one face to the world and burying his true feelings in fantasy, Neil manages to keep his secret. But when fantasy isn't enough and he becomes caught up in the subculture of Dublin's gay nightlife, the pretence must end. The consequences are both hilarious and painful.

Told with honesty, humour and originality, this book brings a new type of hero to modern Irish fiction.

Paperback £5.95

Books for age 13+

THE HEROIC LIFE OF AL CAPSELLA
Judith Clarke

Al Capsella wants to be cool, to fit in with the other teenagers in his neighbourhood. And part of fitting in is to be like all the others – to be "normal". But despite his heroic efforts Al faces a crippling pair of obstacles: his PARENTS.

Along with schoolmates like Louis, Al has his own plans for surviving the abnormal antics of parents, grandparents and teachers. But in the end Al discovers that being really normal is the weirdest thing of all.

Paperback £3.99

AL CAPSELLA AND THE WATCHDOGS
Judith Clarke

Al is nearly sixteen – a very dangerous age according to Mrs Capsella and the other mothers. Known to Al and his friends as the Watchdogs, they stalk the suburbs, ever alert to the perils of parties and other suspect activities.

It's a very trying situation for Al, whose life is already complicated by the unwelcome attentions of Sophie Disher, and a father whose interest in homework borders on the unhealthy.

What's a guy to do?

Paperback £3.99

FRIEND OF MY HEART
Judith Clarke

Daz is in love with Valentine O'Leary, the biggest pig in Mimosa High School. Her brother, William, is in love with a girl he's never spoken to. Eleanor Wand, the music teacher, is in love with the headmaster. Everyone is in love with someone – and doing rather badly. Meanwhile Daz's granny is searching for Bonnie, the long-ago friend of her heart.

Will anyone be successful in the quest for lost friends and true love?

Paperback £3.99

Send for our full colour catalogue